Vidal

OREY GELUS
BOOK THREE

EBONY OLSON

EBANDMUSE
PUBLICATIONS

The Father

VIDAL

SHAKING the rain droplets off my leather jacket, I stepped back inside the nightclub after Sasha and Barden. Sasha's kevlar jeans and boots didn't really fit with the outfits the other clientele were wearing, but her crop top barely covered her boobs. Between the exposed skin and her beauty, no guy was looking at her jeans, including me. If Elisha and Darina weren't on the dance floor flirting and distracting the other male eyes, Sasha would have ended up sandwiched between Barden and me, and the others would have had to take down that vile Execrable.

"I'll just duck into the bathroom and towel down," Sasha told us, then pushed through the door. Savas had her jacket, so her quick exit into the alley behind the club had drenched that measly sash of material across her chest.

Barden and I stopped outside the ladies' and waited. He used his hand to shake the rain from his hair. "You need to visit Valhalla," Barden grumbled. "If you're not staring at her chest, your eyes are glued to her ass."

Huffing in response, I leaned into the wall. Barden wasn't wrong. It'd been a few weeks since I'd gotten laid, and I was horny AF. Seriously, I felt like I'd swallowed a bottle of Viagra this last week. The problem was my cock only wanted one woman in particular.

It wasn't this bad when we first mated. I desired Sasha's happiness and safety, like always, with the addition of my sexual interest in her that developed when she was fourteen. Still, my lust was usually happy being sated anywhere. It was significantly better when I could pull Sasha into their bodies.

The first time had been an accident, but I'd known it the moment it happened. Sasha's lavender-gray eyes looked out at me where, a moment before, they were a vestigial green. When it happened again in Valhalla, it was utterly under my control, something of which Sasha was very aware.

Strangely, being in Sasha's presence was usually enough for our bond. Knowing she was safe and happy satisfied my desire for her for the most part. I certainly wasn't walking around tenting my pants all the time at home with her.

Well, except when the situation called for it. Like when Sasha came out for breakfast, freshly fucked, and wearing nothing but a faded tee and panties. I swear she'd developed some allergy to clothing while we'd been in Elysium, and she wore as little as she could respectfully get away with.

Not that I would complain if she chose to walk around our house naked as the day she was born. Barden and I subconsciously matched Sasha's level of modesty. When she covered herself, so did we. When Sasha was comfortable in panties and a singlet top, boxers or sweats seemed the most I could handle.

Sweeping my fingers through my blond curls, I groaned and stepped away from the wall. I'd also recognized the pattern of Sasha's allergy to clothing and her tendency to need skin-to-skin contact with both of us. She always got very touchy-feely around this time of the month.

I looked pointedly at Barden. He met my eyes without issue.

"You caused this," he reminded, not backing away from the hint of Narsitee in my gaze like others would—especially if they knew what was glaring at them. Barden always had bigger balls than the rest. I'd never seen him flinch.

"She's my mate, and she's ovulating."

Yeah, Sasha was using some form of birth control. I'd asked when we were in Elysium, wanting to know if there was a chance of a baby in the house soon. Whatever she was taking might have stopped her from conceiving, but it didn't stop her cycle. That also meant that Sasha and Barden were at it whenever they could. I'd spent a lot of time out hunting my sister's killer the last few days, and even stayed at my mother's last night.

The look Barden gave me didn't contain any of the possessiveness it did the first time I bit his wife. After that first week of the bond settling, Barden and I warmed to each other. I suspected we were bonded through Sasha in a way. The look he gave me was legitimately empathetic. He could feel how much I wanted to take that final step with our wife, but I'd never push her to make that choice.

Only twice had Sasha given into her instinct with me. The first time I kissed her, which led to me biting her, and then the day we arrived home, she kissed me the same way she kissed Barden. I thought things might shift momentarily, but Sasha pretended it never happened. Acknowledging her feelings for me left her confused, and she would ignore and retreat rather than try to sort through it.

That was six months ago now. Winter was in its last days. The twins were halfway through their first semester of university. The new-look Delta team was working nicely.

The girls lured out the Execrable, and we took them out in a group. Sasha was always with Barden and me. The bond allowed us to communicate with each other. Nash, Savas, Darina, and Elisha typically worked together. Everything was going swimmingly, except my chosen couldn't accept her feelings for me.

"If she just-" I stopped and took a breath. Barden raised a brow, daring me to finish that thought. Huffing, I shook my head. "The primal instinct gets insistent when she's gagging for it."

Barden grunted acknowledgement. He eyed the bathroom door, then me. "We discussed this."

"She sets the lead. I know." That was the agreement when Barden and I talked it out after that initial talk with Sasha. She was so damn innocent that a threesome or polyamory lifestyle didn't even occur to her. I both loved and hated that because it meant she hadn't even considered the alternatives to how this tri-bond could exist.

"She was raised very conservatively, even in comparison to the Orey," Barden reminded me, likely sensing my line of thinking.

My level of frustration hadn't been this bad before. For the most part, I enjoyed what we had. I'd flirt, and Sasha treated me like her best friend. Sasha would hug me, fall asleep, curl against me, tease, and wind me up. Still, for the most part, she was utterly oblivious to any sexual tension between us.

"Even if she was raised Gelus, it wouldn't be any different," I grumbled.

"Unmated Gelus only bond for life if there is a significant connection of the soul. My parents are a rarity. Look at all the other Gelus, you know. Even Gannix never allowed the bond to take with Delila; he loves her."

"Maybe he saw what it did to his mother," I argued.

"Lorka never bonded with Melisandre either. Her abstinence from any other relationship is to punish herself for how she treated Lorka, not because of the bond."

Swallowing, I eyed the dance floor. Occasionally, I forgot how old Barden was. How much experience he had compared to Sasha and me. I wonder if he ever felt trapped in a relationship with children.

"No," Barden answered my thoughts. "Inexperience doesn't mean immaturity. You and Sasha have a lot of power, and the responsibility you both grew up with to control and hide that power from the others made you more mature than your counterparts. Compare Sasha to Elisha or even her brother."

Nodding, I could see what Barden meant. It wasn't like Savas and Elisha were weak. Sasha just had very deadly powers. Just remembering the feel of her power out in the alley tonight, the ease with which she took down the Execrable, got me hard.

"You need to visit Valhalla," Barden grumbled again.

"I know," I agreed as I scanned the club. I wouldn't wait for Valhalla if I found a tall, lean, dark-haired beauty with pale eyes tonight. I'd risk dragging Sasha into it with me. I'd try to protect her. But I wouldn't promise I could keep control. Not with the yearning inside me.

My eyes caught on golden orbs staring back at me from the bar area.

My throat worked as I recognized the face behind those eyes. As soon as we connected, his eyes returned to his Vestigial cover.

Barden was standing straight immediately. "What is it?"

"Take Sasha home," I growled. "Don't argue."

Walking down the steps onto the dance floor, I trusted Barden to make sure our wife wasn't where she shouldn't be and made my way through the throng of bodies to the other side, then to where Savas and Nash were watching for threats.

"How'd you go?" Nash asked. He was still a little unsteady around me. Nash wasn't sure how to deal with the revelation I bonded with Sasha or what that meant. Considering Orey didn't mate, he wasn't sure how to handle the perceived polyamory of our relationship.

"All done. The club's closing in an hour. Barden is taking Sasha home. You should get the girls and travel with them," I suggested. "At the very least, Sasha needs her jacket. It's raining out there."

Finishing his soda, Savas grabbed his jacket and his sister's and spoke to Nash. "You get the girls; I'll meet you outside." Then he headed for the bathrooms. The twins always had a weird sense of where the other was.

"You're not coming?" Nash asked as he picked up Elisha and Darina's jackets.

"I'm meeting up with Simon to keep hunting Yasmine's killer," I dismissed. The others weren't aware I was sating my lust elsewhere. My private life wasn't their business.

"Good luck," Nash said, squeezing my shoulder before he went to tell the girls they were done for the night.

At the bar, I ordered a whiskey and waited. We never drank while working as a team, and alcohol didn't do much for me anyway, but it would look weird if I didn't order something.

"Son." My father joined me once the others were gone.

Already, I could feel Sasha enjoying the ride home.

"Linus," I returned the greeting. I never called him Dad. He wasn't. He'd trained me well, but we had never bonded or talked like a father and son. Plus, we looked the same age and nothing alike. "What are you doing here?"

"Word is you've mated."

How the hell did he know that? "Really?" I chuckled instead.

"At least, we're assuming she's yours, since you are the only permanent resident around this border crossing, and the little witch lives here, too," Linus replied casually. Still, I could feel him watching me closely. Which is why I swallowed my growl at how he referred to Sasha.

"There's been another hanging around enough this last year. He was fucking my sister until he watched her die and did nothing to save her."

"The witches' wombs are sounder for our seed to take. Now that our kind knows that breeding with Gelus and Orey is more likely fruitful, there is no point wasting time with the Vestigials. We're a dying race. Too few of us left. This is why we can't afford to tie ourselves to a chosen one. You are in a unique position with ready access to those girls and hidden by your tie to your mother's blood. You need to sow your seed and breed with as many of them as possible."

This lecture was nothing new. I'd been given the same spiel since my first wet dream. But my father and I differed because I didn't want to sow wild oats willy-nilly. I'd desired Sasha to be my wife and the mother of my children. It was only when Barden arrived and destroyed that possibility that I started screwing every other beautiful woman I encountered.

Seduction came easy to me. It was part of the Narsitee genes. I was so practiced at it now; all I had to do was smile at the woman I wanted, and ten minutes later, I could be buried inside her.

"I should have been a father by now," I muttered. "A Gelus girl took my seed, but one of the witches killed her out of jealousy."

"I heard. Your sister was suspected of the death. It's why her future was cut short." Linus picked up his beer and drank as if that comment wasn't a barb. His lack of empathy always rubbed me the wrong way.

"I'm still going where my lust leads me. I don't need the lecture." I finished my drink. "But I'd like to know who was banging my sister."

"Does it matter? She's the only one you wouldn't touch. She was free for another to try his luck."

There would be no point in using my love for my sister as the reason. "There was insinuation by one of the Crows that the Narsitee fucking with Yasmine was also involved with the Gelus killed by the witch. I'd like to know if it was my child or his."

That made Linus take pause. "I see." Finishing his drink, Linus set the glass down and met my eyes. His were a golden brown. Very different to mine. "I'll enquire the next time I visit my father and see if he knows the answer."

"Thank you." I stood ready to leave.

"In the meantime, you must stop hunting the Narsitee involved with your sister."

Ah, now he reveals why he's here. "Why?"

Linus considered me. "He's strong, Vidal. He doesn't wish to harm you, but he will if you force his hand. And he'll take your little witch as compensation when he's done." He gestured to the barman for another drink. "You may think I'm heartless, but the one you're hunting is much more like the Narsitees of old. I may lack empathy for those with whom I don't have a connection, but I would hate to see the witch who was interesting enough to draw out your need to mate at his mercy."

Gritting my teeth, I glared at the side of my father's head. If I bit and protected Sasha, it would confirm she was my chosen. Right now, it was just a guess on their part.

"The Gelus know a Narsitee was here. They are keeping an eye out. There is only one witch left here now. Your friend would be better off sniffing around some of the clans. This border will be dangerous to him now." Leaning closer, I lowered my voice and let the Narsitee in me come to the surface. "She was my sister. Witch or not. Bitch or not. I shared blood with her, and that bastard used her and culled her. He better hope the Gelus find him first."

Walking away, I strolled onto the dance floor and up to the tall, pale-skinned brunette whose tits were spilling from her halter top. Without touching her, I met her eyes and smiled. She looked me over and gave me the wanton smile I had hoped for. "I'd like to fuck you. Hard."

"I'd love that," she almost panted.

Offering her my hand, I led her to my bike and handed her my helmet.

The Concern

SASHA

IN ONLY MY bra and jeans, I held my top laid out across my hands under the hand dryer in the bathroom while imagining the illicit things I wanted to do to Barden when we got home.

My mood dropped when Vidal's discontent seeped through our bond. For most of our relationship, there had been no jealousy and only the occasional desire for physical intimacy. I'd found that cuddling up to him while we watched television or cooking for him usually satisfied that longing for Vidal, and it made Barden happy, too. Still, this week had been more complex than usual.

A jolt shot down my spine, and I turned and yanked open the door to see what had alerted Vidal. Barden swung into my path, blocking me from exiting the bathroom or seeing behind him.

"Put your top back on, or I will push you back in the bathroom and fuck you on the vanity," Barden growled.

Blinking up at my mate, I quickly glanced down, realized I still had my top in my hands, and was about to expose myself to the entire club. Swallowing, I yanked it over my head and pulled it into place. "What happened?"

"We're leaving," Barden answered.

"Is it another Execrable?"

"No. Vidal would have let the others deal with that."

"Then what is it?"

Grabbing my elbow to stop me from storming through the club, Barden directed me back to the door to the alley. "You're bonded with him. You should feel what the issue is."

"It's hard to push past his sexual frustration right now."

With a grunt in reply, Barden shoved open the back door. "His father is here."

"Jebidiah?" I frowned, unsure what he would be doing in a nightclub.

"His biological father," Barden clarified.

Pausing under the awning to the back door so I wouldn't get drenched again, I blinked up at Barden. Now that I knew the problem, I could sense the heightened emotions. The most troubling was Vidal's fear for me.

The door opened, and Savas joined us, passing me my jacket. "We're done here tonight?"

Barden grunted and then indicated the storm. Savas grinned, closed his eyes, and opened a pathway to our bikes. Once the other three joined us, we made our way two blocks away to where we'd parked.

"I'll take the lead to keep the storm out of our way," Savas directed, and Barden grunted in agreement. "Sasha, come in behind me and push the water off the road as we go so we don't have to slow down."

"I'll take the rear," Nash said as he strapped on his helmet.

There was no point waiting for Barden to volunteer. He wouldn't. He always rode either beside or directly behind me. Vidal usually rode in front of me. That reminder of our missing team member turned my mind to the bond and the hatred he felt for his biological father.

A hand touched my shoulder, snapping my attention to Barden. He handed me my helmet and gestured for me to get on my bike. Before he moved away, he slid his hand down my spine, soothing me even through my jacket. "Let's go home. Vidal needs his space tonight."

Taking a deep breath, I focused on Barden. Our bond was more potent, so it could diminish the link between Vidal and me.

When we got home, there was another distraction to worry about. Setting my helmet in the cubby, we kept our jackets, gloves, and other accessories in; I moaned as liquid heat poured through my veins, pooling in my core.

Taking my elbow, Barden pulled me to him and kissed me deeply, pushing Vidal and his hot makeout session with some stranger to the back of my mind. Barden helped me out of my jacket and wrapped his arms around me to hang it up. I ran my hands all over his chest, clawing him through the material of his shirt as I dragged my hands down and delved under the material so I could feel the ridges and valleys of his sculpted physique.

When my fingers started to work his belt buckle open, Barden groaned, captured my wrists, and spun me around, setting my palms against the cabinet. "Keep your hands here," he murmured in my ear.

Pressing against my back, Barden nibbled the side of my neck and shoulder while he slipped free of his jacket and hung it up. Then he took my hips, directed me back two steps with him, and steered me out of the back door of the garage and into the lift.

Because flying wasn't always an option, and trudging up the mountain was a pain with groceries, Barden and his dad designed a small cable car-style system with an old, repurposed ornate iron lift from the fifties. They'd replaced the cage doors with the glass doors from phone booths to make it weatherproof and connected it to the cable on two sides to keep it stable in high winds. It ran from our garage to the side of our bungalow. It was convenient in wet weather or when I was too worked up and needed to have my hands and mouth on my mate, like now.

As soon as the door closed and Barden had pushed the lever forward to start our ascent, I wrapped my arms around Barden, my mouth tasting every bit of warm flesh I could find.

"I'm so friggin' horny. Please touch me," I pleaded, knowing how much Barden loved me begging. Taking his hand, I guided it down my body, and inside the front of my jeans.

A growl reverberated through Barden's chest as his fingers delved into my panties and stroked through my slick desire. "Fuck, Sash. You are so perfect for me."

"I know," I chuckled around a moan.

"We need to talk about Vidal," Barden muttered. "We can't ignore how he feels. That's not how good relationships work."

"I know. But not right now. He's going to pull me into his fuckery if you don't keep me distracted."

Barden stopped everything and stared at me. "Do you like it?"

"Of course I do, so please keep going."

"No, I meant when Vidal pulls you into the body of the woman he's with."

My eyes opened wide, and then a laugh escaped me as his words sunk in. "No. I much prefer the real thing. It's creepy to be with him like that."

A twitch at the side of Barden's mouth expressed his concern, but I couldn't focus now. I was needy and itching to be touched and fucked. Going up on my toes, I hovered my mouth over Barden's and murmured, "Please!"

A rumble escaped Barden's lips as he pulled me tight against him and kissed the hell out of me. Two bells rang, indicating the lift was about to reach our destination. Barden reached out with one arm and pulled back on the leaver, bringing us to a stop at the side gate to the balcony.

"Jump up," Barden whispered against my lips.

I did as I was told, wrapping my legs around him for him to take me inside. Folding the door open, Barden carried me straight to our bedroom and dropped me on the bed. Before I could sit up, he was yanking my jeans and underwear off my legs. His pants followed.

Climbing over me, Barden settled between my thighs and thrust into me.

I screamed, "Yes."

Barden's cock was directly proportional to his wingspan. Huge. Blinking away tears of relief mixed with a twinge of pain from the violent opening, I held tight as my mate fucked me fast and hard, just like I needed.

That was the thing about Barden. He always knew exactly how I wanted it. The nights I wanted a slow build-up and intense and passionate love-making session. Or like tonight, when I just needed to have my brains fucked out. Barden delivered what I needed every time.

The mate bond worked just as well the other way around. Even before he walked through the door, I could tell if he'd had a difficult night at work and wanted to vent until he fell into an exhausted sleep or when he just wanted to hold me and enjoy being with me.

"Harder. Faster," I gasped.

"Beg for it," Barden grumbled in my ear, not losing momentum in his pounding.

A smile curved the side of my mouth. I'd accidentally discovered Barden liked me begging during my recovery. Now, whenever I was worked up and being demanding, Barden would flip the script and make me beg for what I wanted.

"Please. Barden, please fuck me so hard. I need to feel you so deep inside me that it hurts. I need to come all over your huge—"

With a curse, Barden pulled back, flipped me over, and had me on my hands and knees in my next breath. He drove into me viciously, making me claw at the sheets and cry out.

As soon as my core started throbbing with an impending orgasm, Barden stopped, gripping my hips to stop me from moving as he stayed buried deep inside me. I whimpered and cursed him. Chuckling, Barden lifted his shirt over his head and dropped it to the floor. "Don't worry, Sash, I won't make you wait long."

Rubbing his large palm up my spine, Barden gripped the small sash of my top in his hand and fisted it. "It's almost like you're wearing a harness for me."

"A what—?"

Barden started fucking me again. I was only too happy to egg him on by whimpering, "Yes. Please, fuck me. Don't stop. Barden, please, I need—"

With a curse, Barden slipped his hand between my legs and rubbed my clit. The instant reaction of my body was an explosion through my center as I came screaming his name.

Easing back, Barden pulled out, rolled me onto my back, and captured my mouth in a fiery kiss that zapped straight to my core, making me moan as he simultaneously shoved deep into my body again.

"Please, please, more Barden, please," I pleaded.

Unable to resist, Barden eased back, then thrust back in savagely. A spike of ecstasy burned down my bond with Vidal, letting me know he was about to come, but it was instantly muted by the sheer pleasure of Barden scratching that needy itch inside me.

Over and over, Barden took care of me with a savage passion. Then, as Vidal finally reached his pleasure, my body tightened without warning, and Barden cursed as he lost control. I screamed my orgasm. Barden grunted hard, his cock pulsing his release as my body milked it from him, and somewhere down the bond, Vidal called my name as he trembled and fell to the side of whatever girl he found to fulfill his needs.

Needs a mate should have satisfied. But we were never like that. We had never been more than friends. And yet, as I lay there panting in my mate's arms, I couldn't help but wonder if that were true. A kernel of guilt I'd grown all too familiar with raised its ugly head, but I quickly buried it where it belonged.

It had been over nine months since Vidal bit me. It was far too late to act on those feelings. Nothing could be done. Our relationship was unorthodox enough as it was without making it more complicated by admitting I felt more than just friendship for my other husband.

Groaning, Barden dropped his head to my shoulder, both of us breathing hard. His hand fell away to help keep his weight off me. "Are you happy, Sash?"

"Very. Thank you," I murmured against Barden's neck, my fingertips slicking his sweat-drenched back.

"I didn't mean the sex. I know you enjoyed that. Your cunt is still holding me captive."

Shifting my face, I turned and met Barden's eyes. He stared into mine, and somewhere in that look, I knew he knew where my mind had wandered. He kissed my lips, nose, eyebrow, and forehead. I hugged him tight before he could tell me things had to change. "I'm not ready to talk about it."

Sighing, Barden rolled to the side, taking me with him and wrapping me in his strong arms, cradling me to his chest. "We need to address it, Sash, or it will boil over with no control, and that's how things go to shit. I know you are scared that this tri-bond goes against everything you were raised to believe regarding love and relationships, but for whatever reason, Vidal is also your mate, and the bond took."

Tilting my head back, I met Barden's eyes, the severe intent balanced with his exhaustion. He'd ferried souls all morning and then come home to rest and ended up fucking me all over the house before we had to go on patrol.

"You need to start acknowledging what you feel," Barden continued. "What you were raised to believe should not supersede what you know is true in your heart. Letting society dictate your feelings will destroy you, and I won't let that happen. So, we are going to talk about Vidal, and we're going to do it soon."

He was right. Things were changing. I needed to accept that and figure out how to make that work for all of us. I couldn't fathom how it did, and the idea of Vidal being miserable or leaving us caused tears to well in my eyes. "Not tonight. I'm too tired and don't want to end our night crying because I'm over-emotional."

Holding me tighter, Barden sighed but kissed me again and closed his eyes. "Gelus are possessive of their mates. When Vidal claimed you, my instinct was to kill him, but you stayed my hand. It only took a week for my instinct to pull back and allow him to touch you. No one except your family could get near you like that in my presence, Sash. I didn't want to, but I had to accept that what he claimed was true. It's time you did, too. When Vidal comes home tomorrow, talk to him. Figure out what you both need and then when I get home, we can discuss it together."

My father once told me that choosing not to do the right thing because it was too hard was not a good enough excuse. But how does it work when doing the right thing goes against everything you were raised to expect of yourself and others? I didn't know one person with multiple boyfriends or who cheated to even base a hypothesis on. This was unchartered territory, and I wasn't sure I was brave enough to explore it.

Barden's soft sleep sounds filled the room, but I lay there trying over and over again to understand how I could love two men the way I loved Barden and kept coming up with no answer. Every time I thought of doing anything physical with Vidal, my mind told me it was cheating, and I didn't understand how Barden could be okay with it.

My mind puzzled and rebelled all night long. As morning approached and Barden rolled out of bed to head to Elysia to ferry souls, I accepted that Vidal and I were lost at sea, and I wasn't sure I could ever chart a course to shore.

The Walk of Shame

VIDAL

EXHAUSTED, I landed on the perch of our home. It was still dark out, the sun just hinting at the horizon. Through the French doors, I could see Sasha in the kitchen buttering toast. Barden must have gone to work. Sasha didn't like to sleep alone, so she would get up and study or potter around if neither of us were home. She'd crawled into bed with me several times, but it had to be in the middle of the night, or when Sasha was too exhausted to stay awake for that to happen.

Sweeping a hand through my hair in frustration, I cursed beneath my breath. I needed Barden here to run interference right now. Barden's sympathetic, *'Talk to her,'* swept through my head, making me groan.

"I can't handle this this morning."

'You brought this on yourself.'

"How could I not?"

Avoiding the main doors, I strode along the balcony to the last set of doors, pressed my code to the electric lock, and stepped straight into my bedroom.

'You could have kept your fangs out of my wife. That's how,' Barden replied. The further away he was, the longer the delay.

"She was my mate before she was ever your wife." Grabbing a

19

change of clothes, I went straight for the shower and started the hot water.

'She was mine from the moment I carried her soul to Pandemonium.'

Growling as the response came back while I washed, I slammed my hand against my chest, the wet slap echoing in the bathroom, a flash of pain as I yelled, "I loved her from the moment I set eyes on her. I grew up with her, with the belief she would be mine—then you came and stole her away. I tried to move on. I tried to let her go and let her be happy with you. I tried so fucking hard to give her up and just love her from a distance."

Closing my eyes, I remembered how my heart crumbled when I heard the news. Not for my sister as it should have, but for Sasha and the fear she wouldn't make it. I remembered seeing her so weak her father had to help her walk, the bruising, the pain. I'd felt it even before we'd mated.

Exhaling hard, I leaned on the wall. "I know what you think of Narsitee, and maybe it was selfish, but I love our wife. When her lips touched mine, I knew I was fighting a battle I wouldn't win. I couldn't. So, yes, my desire for her is driving me insane, and I probably deserve this, but can you honestly tell me if she'd chosen me, you could have just walked away?"

Shutting off the shower, I toweled off and yanked on my boxers and jeans. I was cleaning my teeth when an empathetic, *'No.'* Came back from Barden. *'I would have tried my hardest to change her mind, but I wouldn't have forced this on her.'*

Spitting out the paste, I rinsed my mouth. "You say that like I had any control over the moment."

Standing straight, I stared at the mirror and sighed. Really, I couldn't complain. It's not like mating had left me unable to sate my lust elsewhere. It was just becoming harder and harder to be satisfied by anyone who was not my wife.

Back in my bedroom, I noticed a steaming mug of coffee on my chest of drawers. "Shit!" I swept my hand over my face. Snatching up my shirt and jacket, I carried them out to the living area with the coffee and tossed them on the back of the nearest chair. I was meeting Simon in an hour, so there was no point dressing right now.

As I entered the space, Sasha was curled up on the lounge, staring out the window at the river. She quickly swiped her face with the back of her hand and cleared her throat.

Pausing, I assessed our bond, and my stomach hollowed. I opened my mouth, stopped, took a moment, and said, "I didn't mean for you to hear that. I'm tired and frustrated and wasn't in the mood for Barden's lecture this morning."

"I know. I can feel it," Sasha replied.

Taking a breath, I moved around to the lounge and sat beside her. Setting my coffee on the table, I took her hand and held it while we stared out the window.

"I'm not saying I'm unhappy with what we have. Seventy-nine percent of the time, I couldn't be happier with our setup. Fifteen percent of the time, I'd be happier if I could kiss you without making you go all weird and shy around me for days afterward. The other five, I wish I could have the same type of relationship with you that Barden does."

"What about the other one percent?" Sasha asked quietly, having done the math in her head.

Smirking, I squeezed her hand. "I want to crawl into bed with you and Barden, and all three of us be together intimately." Sasha blinked wide eyes at me. I shrugged. "Threesomes are more common than you realize."

The innocence of my wife was mind-blowing and something I adored about her. It's not that I wanted to corrupt her. It wasn't about fucking. I wanted to be free to love my wife and to worship her like she deserved to be worshiped. I may have been a Narsitee, but Sasha was my Goddess.

Silence hung between us, but the conflicting emotions and morals Sasha was struggling with were like a heavy metal band slashing their guitars with the amp at its highest volume in the same room as us.

"I'm not trying to pressure you into anything. I know you are doing what feels right for you and that you are confused by this throuple thing we have going. I'm not adding to that dilemma for you. You overheard and felt my frustration, and I'm just clarifying where that is coming from. You're ovulating right now, making you harder to resist than usual."

Sasha winced as if I pinched her. "Seriously? Is nothing private between us? You know where my cycle is up to?"

Smirking at the disgust on her face, I leaned in close. "Yes, and so does Barden. And unlike me, he loves it. I would, too, if it meant you were climbing in my lap every chance you got."

Cheeks and chest flushing bright red, Sasha bit her lip and hid her face. "God!"

My magic sprinkled down my spine. "Yes?"

She threw an elbow at me, I caught it with a laugh, then shifted as I tackled her to the lounge and started tickling her. Sasha screeched and laughed, trying to fight me off, but subconsciously opened her legs to welcome my body between them so that by the time we were panting and trying to recover, I was lying over her, my hardening cock pressing against her pelvis.

And in a testament to just how relaxed she was around me, Sasha didn't even blink at the position. Not until I cupped her face and swiped my thumb over her bottom lip. Her eyes widened, her pupils dilated, and her hands suddenly found my shoulders. The desire in her warring with her loyalty to Barden whipped up that tornado of confusion in her mind.

"Just say the word, and I'm all yours, baby." I dropped a peck to her luscious mouth, then pulled back, getting myself up and away from her and forcing a smile. "But not right now. Simon's waiting for me." A slight fib to cover for my quick withdrawal.

Grabbing the coffee, I pretended not to see how Sasha closed her eyes and swallowed hard at my departure. I also had to turn quickly and try and convince myself not to notice that she was only wearing panties and my fucking college hoodie that I'd left on the kitchen bench yesterday after I got home. *Fuck me!* Temptation, thy name is Sasha Tormen.

Walking into the kitchen, I drank my coffee and tried to bring the light-hearted fun back between us. "Have you thought about hyphening our names?"

"Huh?" Sasha eased herself up to sitting.

"Well, you're married to two guys, so you can't just take Barden's surname. You'll have to take mine too. Sasha Assion-Reid has a nice ring to it, don't you think?"

Rolling her eyes, Sasha fell back on the couch. "Unless someone puts a ring on my finger, it'll stay Tormen."

"Oh, baby, you needn't have made it so easy." Leaving the mug on the sink, I searched in my jacket pocket and found my grandma's ring that my mother gave me just yesterday. Surprising Sasha, I grabbed her hand and had it on her ring finger before she even realized what was happening. "Sasha Reid, it is."

While Sasha blinked at the white gold and pink sapphire engagement ring on her finger, I snatched up my shirt and jacket and quickly left for the door.

"Wait, Vidal, what is this?" Sasha murmured, staring at the ring, her breathing picking up as she started to freak out, which was not the reaction I expected. I thought she'd laugh it off like she always did when we played pranks on each other. But the bond was pure shock, love, and a little fear. "Vidal?"

Not wanting to analyze why the ring caused such a reaction in Sasha, I spread my wings and jumped from the ledge when she followed me out.

"Wait, why won't it budge? Vidal, why can't I take it off?" she called after me as I glided towards the backdoor to the new garage addition for my bike. "I'll kick your ass!"

Finally, there was the response I expected.

Laughing openly now, I landed, furled my wings, and stepped into the add-on garage we'd built to house our bikes when we moved in. It was recessed to the main garage and had an extra storage space at the back for anything we didn't want to keep in the house.

I'd just got my shirt and jacket on and thrown a leg over my bike when Sasha stormed into the garage in nothing but her panties. She must have yanked my hoodie off to unfurl her wings quickly. Trying not to stare at Sasha's naked body, I focused on the missing clothing. "You better not have lost that jumper in the trees."

Ignoring me, breathing heavily, Sasha held up her hand, now bearing my claim of ownership. "What the fuck, Vidal?"

"You don't like it?" I asked nonchalantly. "Mum gave it to me yesterday to give to you. It was my grandmother's, and she'd left it to me for when I wanted to marry. Since I married you, it technically is yours now."

"And you just decided to shove it on my finger without any explanation?" Sasha screeched. She was so fucking sexy standing there in just her panties, face and chest red in her rage, my cock was hard as a rock and ready to burst from my jeans at any minute.

"Well, you said you wouldn't change your name without one," I justified with that easy-going smile.

Sasha stormed closer. "And why can't I take it off?"

"Well, I don't want Barden having a tantrum about me beating him to it and tossing it out the door. Just safeguarding a family heirloom."

Slamming her hands to my chest, Sasha gripped my shirt. "That's bullshit!"

Fuck, I was too tired to do this. It was meant to be a way to lighten the moment, but I should have known beforehand, with the tension of the conversation, that it wouldn't fly. Sick of being the nice guy, I let Sasha see how I felt.

"No, bullshit is that I just got through telling you how badly I desire you, making sure I didn't cross the line with you and leaving to prevent it, only to have you chase after me naked and press yourself up against me."

Sasha blinked, glanced down at her body, and turned pink everywhere as she tried to back off.

Too late, princess!

Gripping her wrists to hold her to me, I didn't let her back down. "Tell me what you want, Sasha. You lean into me, rub up against me, crawl into my bed, but then play coy and back away a moment later. I've given you space. I've promised to let you take the lead in how this will work. I've followed your cues at every turn and been the understanding boyfriend who will forever play second fiddle to the first preference. What do you want from me?"

Staring back at me with wide eyes, Sasha opened her mouth but looked just as lost as always. "I... I don't—"

"Do you want me to be the bad guy here?" I asked. "Do you need me to make the first move so you can decide whether you want me or not, so you can tell Barden that I forced your hand in this as well?"

Sasha blinked. "No, I..."

Her words said one thing, but her heart started beating quickly when I offered to take the fall. Her body heated, and her nipples tightened. Even down the bond, she screamed her interest in what I had just offered.

'Barden!' I pleaded for his guidance, permission, and sudden appearance to stop us from going beyond a point of no return. Because if I acted on her response just now, there would be no coming back from it. I would change our relationship irrevocably. For better or worse, I wouldn't know until it was done.

I reeled Sasha closer, wrapped one arm around her waist, and threaded the other into her hair to fist the long, silky strands at the back of her head, giving me utter control over her.

"Vidal," Sasha breathed, her pupils dilated with need.

"Tell me no," I pleaded. "Tell me to get out and never to come back. Make your choice, Sasha. Love me or don't."

Tears overflowed her lavender-grey eyes, her fingers gripping my shoulders, her nipples pebbled where they pressed against my chest. Closing the distance, I kissed her hard, releasing years of yearning into that kiss. Her lips were salty with her emotions, but her mouth tasted of chocolate and coffee, and my everything. This girl was my eternity.

Combing her fingers up my neck, Sasha gave as good as she took. Shifting her balance, she leaned into me, rubbed her body against mine, and moaned for me.

Shifting my arm at her waist, I slipped my hand into her panties and brushed the seam of her sex, spreading her to find her drenched for me. Groaning, I pressed my middle finger inside her, found her trigger, and started rubbing it.

Panting, Sasha kissed me harder. Her hands pulled up my shirt until she could get her hands beneath it to feel my flesh, and then she lifted herself onto me, straddling me where I sat astride my bike. Her hands unbuckled my belt and were yanking at the button on my jeans when I snatched both her wrists and pinned them behind her back.

"Tell me you want this," I pleaded. "Tell me you want me?"

Breathing heavily, Sasha's eyes were glassy with want, her body rocking against the hard bulge in my jeans in the absence of my fingers, but she couldn't say the words. The more I longed for them, the more she cried. Sasha's body and heart were screaming 'yes', but her morals wouldn't let her go.

It fucking broke me. Dropping my head to her chest, I held her pinned while I forced my desire to back away. To protect my heart and protect her, I had to lock what I felt for her down.

"Vidal," Sasha sobbed, no doubt feeling my withdrawal down the bond. "I'm sorry."

Releasing Sasha gently, I kept my head bowed as I eased her off my lap and used the reach of my arms to set her away from me. Swallowing down the pain of a mate's rejection, I grabbed my helmet, pulled it on, and then hit the button to open the garage door.

"Vidal," Sasha whispered, her hand reaching for me.

Grabbing her wrist to stop her from touching me, my gut twisted as I eased my ring from her finger, releasing the holding spell. Sasha's sobs grew louder as I turned her hand, placed the ring in her palm, and closed her fist around it. "I meant what I said. It's yours to keep."

Pushing out of the stand, I avoided looking at Sasha again, my heart feeling shredded in my chest as I sped out of the garage. It was my own fault. I should have let the status quo stand as it always had. Why couldn't I today?

"Vidal, please!" Sasha called as I raced down the driveway.

They knew about her. My father and the one I was hunting knew Sasha was my mate, and they'd threatened to take her from me. For whatever reason, Sasha was still open to my bite after she mated with Barden, so she could potentially be bitten by one of them. Until we consummated our bond, she was susceptible.

'You okay, brother?' Barden finally responded.

Asshole probably watched me crash and burn while shoveling popcorn in his mouth. Shaking my head, I hit the button for my music and focused on getting to the Milkbar.

The Breaking

SASHA

MY HEART SPLINTERED. "VIDAL," I whispered, reaching for him, wanting him to understand I just needed time to talk this through with the both of them, to know how this tri-bond could give everyone what they needed and still make everyone happy like it had six months ago. What had changed so drastically in the last twenty-four hours?

Grabbing my wrist, Vidal prevented me from touching him. My stomach hollowed as Vidal eased the engagement ring from my finger. I wasn't even upset about the ring, just how it was delivered. Such a Vidal way to propose, shit-stirring me as usual, but on the tail of his revelation about his unhappiness in our relationship, it was too much.

My heart cracked again, splintering like an old wooden fence as Vidal turned my wrist, placed the ring in my palm, and curled my fingers around it. "I meant what I said. It's yours to keep," Vidal murmured without looking at me.

Pushing out of the stand, he sped out of the garage, leaving me there with my chest cracking open and my insides twisted in knots. "Vidal, please!" I screamed as he raced away from me. "Vidal," I pleaded for him to come back, because I knew if he didn't turn around now, he wouldn't.

That was the last thing I felt before the bond went dark between us. That he saw me as his weakness. The splinters in my chest pierced my lungs, making it impossible to breathe properly. My knees buckled, causing me to crouch over them, hugging them tight as I tried to fill the space inside me that was left in the absence of my bond with Vidal.

"Sasha," my dad called as he rushed into the garage's back door. Peering up at him through my tears, Dad's face fell. "Oh, Sash." Yanking his shirt over his head, he gently put it over mine, then eased each arm into a sleeve to cover me. "Couples fight. Adding a third to the mix... Considering how it started, I don't know how things have gone as smoothly as they have for you three this long."

When he picked me up in a fireman hold, I wrapped my arms around his neck and sobbed into his shoulder. "It hurts," I whimpered.

Nuzzling my hair, Dad kissed my head as we stepped outside. "This is why I never allowed the bond to develop with your mother," he confessed. Then his big white wings stretched out behind him, and we lifted into the air.

Considering how volatile his relationship with my mother was, I could imagine how traumatic it would have been had there been the sort of bond I had with Vidal, let alone the breathing-pulsing life bond with Barden.

Walking onto our landing with a grace I was still to muster, Dad set me on the sofa. Stepping back outside, he snatched up Vidal's jersey, then slid the door closed to block out the cold wind blowing through the canyon. The place was freezing after I'd left the door open. Thanks to the underfloor heating, it wouldn't take long to heat up again. Still, I pulled the throw rug off the back of the lounge to cover my legs and cuddled into it.

"How did you cope with Mum leaving you?" I asked as Dad busied himself in the kitchen.

"Well, we don't have the bond, so there was only the emotional pain," Dad answered. He joined me on the sofa and set a cup of tea in front of me before sitting with his coffee. "I guess the only way is to keep on breathing. Is that what happened? Vidal has left you?"

"I don't know. It feels like it," I sobbed once, held my breath, and forced myself not to break. *Just breathe.*

"I doubt it will be for long, Sash. Gelus..." Dad shook his head, rethinking his words. "You are bonded with your mates. It makes it nearly impossible to leave one another. It's not just an emotional but physical and, dare I say, spiritual connection that you've formed. You can't just say 'nope' and walk away from that."

Sniffling, I cringed. "What if you've never been physical? What if you've never taken it that far? Can they leave then?" *What if they're not just a Gelus or Orey but something much more dangerous?*

Considering me, Dad put his hand on my knee. "When I said physical, I didn't mean sex, Sash. The joining of bodies cements a bond, but you and Barden were physically bound from the first kiss. He told me that was all it took for the bond to lock."

I remembered that first kiss and how I could sense Barden's nearness afterward. That sense grew stronger with every interaction until we finally married—the Gelus way.

"It was the same for Vidal, though he took it further and bit you." Dad shook his head. "I'm still confused by the mauling and, frankly, disturbed, but Barden assured me that's a common way of claiming one's mate so that everyone can see it."

"Vidal didn't have control in that moment," I defended. "He didn't intend to bond with me. He just wanted to know what I saw under the bridge. Once we kissed, the mating took a life of its own, and Vidal was a slave to his instinct. I know he didn't mean to do it. It was the first thing I felt when the bond formed."

Studying me, Dad squeezed my knee. "You think that reluctance plus the failure to consummate the bond enables Vidal to leave you if he chooses to?"

"Doesn't it?" I asked. Pressing my hand to my stomach, I couldn't stop my eyes from overflowing with the inner turmoil and pain of his absence. "I feel hollow. He blocked the bond somehow. He told me I had to make a choice. Love him, or don't. When I hesitated, he chose for me."

My heart trembled in my chest, remembering the hurt in Vidal's eyes, and I sobbed anew. "But I do love him, Dad. I do. I just don't know how that works with two mates. I don't know how to do this, but I love them both."

Dad's strong arms wrapped around me and pulled me against his chest, rocking me as I cried my heart out. "You're so young," Dad murmured, kissing my head as he rocked me.

"You were so innocent when you jumped headfirst into a full-blown relationship with Barden. You were thrown into this tri-bond only months later without any prewarning or discussion on how it would work. The boys should have discussed this with you as soon as it happened. They shouldn't have let you take the wheel without any guidance."

"I thought Vidal was happy with how we were," I told him, trying to understand how we ended up here.

"Did you? Or were you ignoring the hints that he needed more because it made you uncomfortable?" Dad pressed gently. "This can't have been out of the blue, Sash."

The truth of his words smashed into me, flooding me with guilt, and the last thread holding me together snapped. Clinging to my dad, I fell apart.

Cursing, Dad held me tighter and rubbed my back, trying to soothe me as I wallowed in my misery. The door opened, but I was lost in my despair and guilt.

"Dad?" Savas asked.

"I've got her. Call Barden and see how far away he is."

The door closed again, and I clung tighter to my father. Barden's words from last night played in my head.

'It will boil over with no control, and that's how things go to shit.'

Well, Barden was right about that.

A cool breeze kissed my cheek, and then the door slid closed.

"She's asleep," Dad whispered as Barden lifted me from my dad's hold. I curled into him, hiding my tear-stained face. I'm sure I looked like shit and had never liked anyone to see me after I ugly cried.

"She cried herself to sleep while I held her. Been a long time since my daughter has needed her father like that." There was a tenderness coating frustration in his voice I hadn't heard since I'd nearly died beside Yasmine.

"Did she talk to you?" Barden murmured.

"Yes."

I don't know what passed between them, but Barden grunted and carried me to our bedroom. I clung to him when he tried to put me on the bed. Grunting in a way that soothed me, I let go and rolled away so that my back was to the room, and I could stare out the window as silent tears continued to mar my face.

Barden admonished me privately down the bond for even thinking I could hide my emotions from him, but he didn't say anything in front of my dad or brother. Once I'd curled in on myself under the throw blanket still covering me, Barden sat beside me and rubbed my back.

The tap ran in the bathroom, and Savas said, "Here. She cried a lot. I hate seeing her like this."

"Just because I wasn't here doesn't mean I missed it," Barden grumbled. He leaned over me and handed me a wet face cloth to clean my face. "I'm sorry I took so long," he murmured. "I had a soul on board and was across the other side of Pandemonium. I used the gates to get back here as quickly as possible."

The gates were like the veils that were portals between Elysia and Pandemonia but also allowed you to travel between continents and cities in each realm. Barden took me through one when we were in Elysia to get to Paris but explained the Narsitee created the gates, and the feel of their magic always made him uncomfortable. He usually preferred to take the time to fly to a veil rather than use a gate.

Barden expected me to feel sickened by the gate's power like most Gelus and Orey, but it hadn't bothered me. We concluded that was probably because of my bond to a Narsitee hybrid.

"We should go," Dad said.

"No wisdom to impart this time, Gannix?" Barden said as if in challenge.

"You are older than me and have been amid this tri-bond for nine months. You know what needs to happen. You were hoping you wouldn't have to. Avoidance only made it worse than it needed to be."

Grunting in acknowledgment, Barden placed his hand on my hip and squeezed. "I may have more life experience, but I've never had to navigate the perilous path of a relationship complicated by innocence and fear."

"The only thing my daughter has ever feared is disappointing those she loves. Assure her that her instinct is not guiding her wrong, and it will cure at least one of those issues." Dad paused momentarily and then grumbled, "Probably both of them."

Savas snickered, and I could feel Barden's humor down the bond.

"Will we see you at dinner?" Dad asked as they headed for the door.

Barden grunted an affirmative, then as the door closed behind them, Barden curled around me from behind, holding me tight. "Vidal will come back. You know he's scared by whatever his father said last night. We'll find out what that was and put his mind to rest, and he'll come home."

Staring out the window across our covered pool to the range on the other side of the canyon, I didn't argue with what Barden said. He was right. Once we knew what scared Vidal, we could counter it, and he'd come home. What neither of us acknowledged at this moment—but hung in the bond like a wet gym sock with a tennis ball knotted inside—was that there was no going back to the relationship we had before today.

'Make your choice, Sasha. Love me or don't.'

There was no coming back from those words. From that kiss. From how it felt to finally give in to my instincts and be intimate with Vidal, the way I'd been tempted to for several months now.

The Bad Boyfriend

VIDAL

PARKING my bike around the back, I came in the back door. Hawk eyed me, then gave me a nod of greeting. To the Gelus, I was still an Orey, but I was working with them to hunt a mutual enemy, so they'd accepted me on some level. Or maybe it was my weird throuple status with Barden and Sasha that made them willing to let me into their community.

My chest ached. Rubbing my sternum, I blocked out Sasha and refused to think about how I left her.

"You okay, man? You look a little peaky," Falco asked as I passed him entering the kitchen.

"I'll tell you about it when Simon gets here," I muttered, sweeping a hand through my hair, scruffing it like I wished I could shake my feelings loose.

Falco frowned. "Can I get you something?"

"If you have whisky, I'd love it. Otherwise, coffee and food would be good, thanks."

The breakfast rush was starting. Because it was Sunday and we lived in a god-fearing town, many citizens would go to church and then come here or to the restaurants on the other side of Canyon Falls on their way home.

When I was feeling a little blue, I usually attended church. All that praying was like super vitamins to my health and power. After the morning I had, I was craving that sort of uplift. Maybe after I'd met with Simon, I'd hit up the late-morning mass. It was always the more attended mass anyway.

If I was super lucky, there might be a pale-skinned, pale-eyed brunette in attendance I could lure into the confessional for some more meaningful prayer and deal with the semi I was still sporting for my wife.

Fuck, if I didn't long for her so badly right now. Sliding into the booth Sasha had all but claimed as hers, I dropped my head to the table and groaned. Sasha's psyche was bashing against my consciousness, trying to be acknowledged, and Barden was there, lurking. It was the first time I resented the bond. The first time I regretted losing control and claiming Sasha as my chosen.

No. Wrong word. I'd never regret it. The last nine months had been some of the best in my life. My bondmates knew my secret and accepted me. Loved me—as a friend.

Like a fucking brother! As Barden had reminded me.

My thumb rubbed across my lips. Sasha was a vicious kisser. So full of passion and want. I was addicted from that first time. Having just got another hit, I was craving more of that high.

Why am I doing this to myself?

It was a stupid question. I knew why. I had from the moment I sank my teeth into her neck. I was in love with her. I had always loved Sasha since we met when she was six. Sighing, I wiped my hand down my face and sat back.

"Long night?" Falco asked as he set a coffee and plate of scrambled eggs, french toast, sausage, hash, and bacon in front of me, alongside a bowl of porridge with fresh fruit. Falco had a knack for knowing how hungry someone was and what they needed to get through the day. I hadn't ordered from the menu for half a decade. I just told him if I was hungry or thirsty and let him put what I needed in front of me.

"Haven't made it to bed yet." Picking up the coffee, I smirked after the first sip. "You're awesome," I told Falco as I sipped the whisky-laced coffee.

Giving me a wink, he eyed the door as the first of the breakfast rush pushed through it. "Our morning staff should be here in thirty. Don't share anything juicy with Simon before we join you."

"You mean about the hunt or the fact I can still smell my wife on my fingers from this morning?" I teased. I then made the mistake of sucking that finger into my mouth. God, the taste of Sasha. I'd never tasted her like that before, and now my cock was hard again, and my need for her was crippling.

"Woah, dude, are you okay?" Falco stared wide-eyed as I snarled at the pain clawing open my insides.

Gripping the table, I breathed through the agony of leaving my chosen. I couldn't go back. Not after I'd laid my feelings on the table and Sasha rejected me. It would have been one thing if she'd stayed behind and thought on it. Let us take a breather, consider what I put out there, and then tell me where she stood. Coming after me like that... forcing my hand.

Hanging my head, I held in a whimper of pain. I'd caused it with the ring. I didn't mean to give it to her like that—I wasn't going to go down on one knee for her, either. I planned to offer it to her as a gift with some words about how, as my wife, it was hers. Her reaction to changing her name stirred me up, and I couldn't help but play with her. Maybe if I hadn't just dumped my needs at her feet, she would have laughed it off, but it happened how it did.

"Do you ever feel like every time you try and do the right thing, you just continuously fuck it up?" I asked no one as I slumped in my seat.

"It's called the folly of youth," Falco laughed. I'd forgotten Falco was still there. Giving me a pat on the shoulder, Falco gave me a reassuring smile. "She'll forgive you." He headed off to start taking orders.

"I'm not sure forgiveness is what is needed this time," I muttered to myself. Shaking my head, I sat up, pulled the porridge to me, and ate the healthy breakfast before digging into the protein-rich fry-up.

By the time Simon slid into the booth opposite me, I had finished my food and enjoyed the coffee.

"You look like shit," Simon acknowledged as he made a gesture to Falco.

I huffed and held my empty cup up to Falco, hoping for a second helping. "I ran into something not so Vestigial last night. Something more along the lines of what we've been hunting."

"You deal with it?"

"Spoke with it," I answered casually. Other than the Assions, my secret was entirely protected. Even Savas and Gannix only knew part of my truth.

Cocking a brow, Simon sat back. "What'd it have to say?"

"My sister's lover knows we're hunting him, and he's watching me." Letting Simon absorb that, I waited for Falco to put two more coffees in front of us, this one sadly lacking the extra emotional support. Falco and Hawk joined us as I met Simon's eyes. "He knows about Sasha and me and told this friend if I don't back off, he'll take her." I sipped the hot coffee while Simon just stared at me.

"Who knows?"

"The Narsitee we're hunting," I told them.

The brothers cursed. After a moment, Simon sat forward. "Wait, you ran into some random Elysian, and they just offered that tidbit?"

"No, they came looking for me. I've known him a while, but I don't much like him, so I don't seek him out," I clarified. "My sister's lover thought he'd make a good messenger for me."

"Back off, or he'll take your wife next time?" When I nodded, Simon cursed. "Have you told Sasha and Barden?"

"Barden wasn't home when I arrived, and Sasha and I..." Blowing out a breath, I slumped back. "Let's just say I'm in the doghouse." When the Gelus lifted their brows at me, I shrugged. "I let the fear of that bastard getting his hands on her direct my behavior."

Shaking his head, Simon sipped his coffee. He was the older of the three. I could tell by the way they always let him direct the conversation. Or maybe it was his standing as Lorka's second. After a moment, he said what I knew was coming. "You need to back off. Let us handle it. Hawk, Falco and I have no one he can come after to hurt us."

Scoffing, I replied without thinking. "You have a sister. Don't be naive. They're targeting Orey and Gelus girls for breeding. Elisha is probably already on his watch list."

Simon's head shot up, his eyes meeting mine. "What did you just say?"

Swallowing, I realized what I had revealed and could have kicked myself. Instead, I kept that mask of lazy cockiness I'd had in place most of my life and acted like it wasn't news. "Became obvious to me after what happened with Sophie." Sitting forward, I stared into the heterochromia eyes of the Gelus opposite me. "And to answer you, I'm not backing off. Sasha can handle herself. The last six months on the team have proven that."

"Execrable are not Narsitees," Simon reminded.

"The only reason Sasha's life was endangered the first time she came face-to-face with five Execrable was because of her friends. I know my wife's power. Trust me, had Sasha been by herself, she would have taken all five out in one move and walked away, barely affected. Sasha may be kind-hearted and innocent, but she's a vicious little thing when she needs to be."

My mind turned to Athur Nellaf and the fate she had decided for him without any hesitation or regret. Sasha may have looked like a heavenly angel, but if you'd told me she had a few drops of Narsitee in her blood, I'd have believed it without question.

Sasha didn't hesitate to mete out justice when she felt it was called for and showed no mercy. Then again, having known her mother as long as I had, maybe that was just the Orey in her. Fuck knows Mia and her mum turned out to be real pieces of work, and they were as Orey as they came.

Assessing me, Simon pulled out his phone and started texting. "Who are you contacting?" I asked.

"Barden. This affects him, and he's the most experienced when it comes to dealing with those sociopaths," Simon answered.

"He's busy dealing with the fallout of my morning," I admitted, the guilt of leaving Sasha naked and crying like that gnawing at my heart. "Give him a few hours."

The brothers eyed me, then got up. "We need to do some work. Give us thirty to clear out the morning rush, and we'll plan the next hunt," Hawk excused.

Eyeing me, Simon set his phone aside and waited for the brothers to be busy. "That bad, hey?"

"Be glad I'm not halfway into a bottle of Johnny right now." Picking up my coffee, I made a plan to drown my emotions in something with a high alcohol content after the next hunt was done. Until then, I needed my senses. Checking the time, I smirked at Simon. "Want to go to church?"

"What?" He nearly spat his coffee laughing.

I shrugged. "If I was a narcissistic god, it's where I'd be hanging out."

Considering that, Simon pursed his lips. "Good point. But no. All that worship crap rubs me the wrong way. If their god existed, he wouldn't be hanging around in a building enjoying blessing them. He'd be watching those practicing what they preach by feeding the homeless at the missions and shelters or standing by the people who donate their time to Doctors without Borders."

Shrugging a shoulder, I didn't argue. "True, but a Narsitee may still be prowling. Barden said that worship shit is right up their alley. I'll check the church out on my way home."

"Do you even know what you're looking for?" Simon teased, but there was a serious note to his words.

"I'm going to go out on a limb and guess the asshole standing there looking like he's getting high." Like I did when I attended mass.

Picking up his coffee, Simon nodded in agreement. "Good point. Call me if you see that, and we'll check it out."

Thank God I couldn't see myself. "Will do. Any other ideas for the next hunt?"

"Plenty, but let's wait for the brothers to return."

Happy with that and having bought cover in case I was seen going to the church, I signaled Falco for another coffee and pleaded for some of the laced stuff with my eyes before I allowed myself to connect back into my bonds.

'Is she okay?' I asked Barden.

'About as much as you are, asshole.'

Yeah, I expected that.

Sighing down the bond, Barden dropped the anger. *'Give her time.'*

Already planning to give Sasha some space, I didn't object. What I hated about the request was the same thing I disliked about my decision. Time and space were eternal.

The Window

SASHA

BARDEN'S PHONE buzzed on the kitchen bench. I was finally dressed for the day, and Barden had pulled me in to snuggle with him on the sofa while we had brunch.

Tilting my head back, I smiled up at my husband. "You should get that."

Shoving another spoon of the peanut butter chia pudding I'd made for us into his mouth, Barden pulled himself up from behind me and strode into the kitchen. He only wore tracksuit pants, so the view of his sculpted back was divine, and my body was filled with need.

Vidal had said I was ovulating, but honestly, there was never a time I didn't desire Barden since I first developed a sexual interest in the opposite sex. And by that, I meant Barden. It had always been Barden. Frowning at that thought, I remembered hanging out with the Orey boys before Barden came to town. Had it always only been Barden, or had I had some semblance of attraction to the other guys?

I hadn't paid much attention to the boys back then other than learning to use my powers by watching them train.

"Who did you watch the most?" Barden asked.

Looking up, I found Barden standing before me, one of his eyebrows cocked. "What do you mean?"

"Before I came along and stole the limelight, who did you watch the most to learn your powers?" Barden pressed while typing out a response on his phone.

Thinking about it, a knot formed in my throat. "Vidal. Even when he was sitting and watching the others, my eyes were always drawn to Vidal. I liked the ease with which he could throw his power around. I could tell he was holding back; more was hidden beneath the surface. He only put in effort when Savas challenged him to meet his level, and then he'd rise to meet him but never surpass him. Watching Vidal is how I learned to hide my ability."

Standing there watching me, I could feel Barden pressing me to recognize what my attraction was down the bond. It was subtle, not an outright telling, but because I was overly sensitive today, I could pick up on the tendrils of him trying to get me to come to terms with my true feelings; that the reason I had never looked at anyone else before Barden arrived was because Vidal had my attention.

That's when I noticed Barden had changed into jeans and had a shirt and jacket on the table. "You're going out?"

"Simon wants me to meet up with him and Vidal to discuss whatever Vidal was told last night."

Clenching my teeth, I threw the blanket off and got to my feet. "He told Simon but not me." Shaking my head, I stormed into the kitchen and washed the mason jar.

"Vidal's behavior this morning directly correlates to whatever his father told him last night. He's scared by something; I felt that much down the bond. Then he came home thinking about whatever that was, and I didn't guard my emotions well enough and fell right into his chaos when I wanted to talk to him about our relationship and put him at ease."

"Sash—"

"No, this was my fault. Vidal was looking for a way to push me away, and instead of telling us what happened, he drove me into a situation I wasn't ready to be in. I crossed a line I wasn't ready to, and when he did the honorable thing and made sure I wanted what I was offering, and I hesitated, he took it as me rejecting him," I ranted.

Tears cascaded down my cheeks, the misery and heartache of this morning still a fresh wound. "I wasn't. I just wasn't ready. I wanted the three of us to discuss what we all need. I needed us to all be open and discuss how this would work, and I messed it up by reacting."

Wrapping me in his arms as I cried against his chest again, Barden held me tight. "You were both overtired and deep in your feelings. It was bound to happen, Sash. But Vidal will calm down, and we can talk it out when he comes home."

Lifting my chin, Barden forced me to meet his eyes. "And just so you know, I'm not angry for what happened between you this morning. I've been expecting that line to get crossed since I accepted Vidal as your other mate."

"You have?"

Inhaling, Barden grunted affirmation. "I've had months to witness you bonding, both of you, and getting comfortable with you touching, cuddling up together, and even you crawling into bed with him when I'm not home. I'm surprised Vidal's taken this long to lose his cool. Again, I think that was mostly because of what was said last night."

Hanging my head, I felt terrible. "I messed up. You told me to talk to him, to follow my instincts, and I hesitated." Swiping away the tears, I shook my head. "I wanted it, but my head kept telling me it was wrong. That it would be cheating on you. We never agreed to this. That day we sat in my dad's office, he said he'd be my friend, that he just needed to know I was safe and happy, and you only accepted the bond because he said he didn't need me that way."

Bending his knees to be eye level with me, Barden cupped my face. "Sash, that was the first day. The bond hadn't fully settled, and I'd barely connected with him then. Within weeks of that happening, the bond between us was a different creature. It had grown into something even I could never have expected. Surely you felt that?"

"I did, but you never said... Vidal never asked for..." Words failed me as I stared at my mate, begging him to understand. Feeling the love between us didn't undo the words that were spoken.

Huffing, Barden slammed his mouth to mine, kissing me until I was panting for oxygen and my body had melted against his.

Pulling back, Barden waited for me to open my glazed eyes and let the lust fog clear enough to hear him. "This is my fault. I wanted to let you drive this tri-bond however you were comfortable. I should have recognized that you needed a navigator to guide you through the unfamiliar landscape."

Caressing his shoulder, I kissed his pec and rested my head over his heart. "It's not like you have done this before, either."

Barden grunted and combed his fingers through my hair.

"I guess I should look up some threesome porn and see if that appeals," I murmured.

Groaning, Barden dropped his forehead to mine. "Not yet. Let's sit down with Vidal; then, you two should work towards being comfortable with intimacy between you before we go all out on the tri-bond."

Biting my lip, I considered what that would feel like and told Barden, "I'd rather you be involved. It would feel wrong not having you there."

Barden grunted in disagreement. "Trust me, having someone watching you be intimate the first time is far from comfortable. Unless you're into exhibitionism, which neither of us is." Barden lowered his mouth to my ear, saying, "If you feel guilty afterward, I will happily let you beg for forgiveness." He squeezed my ass and stole another kiss, leaving me breathless and needy when he pulled away. "But I have to go. I told Simon I'd find Vidal and meet him at his place."

Huffing in annoyance, I yanked the plug out of the sink. "He's at church."

That made Barden stop and assessed me. "How do you know that? I can sense him, but not what he's doing."

"It's the power-up. I feel it through the bond, even with him choking it. It is like this zing up my spine that makes me all tingly as the service goes on. I've felt it a couple of times before when he's gone to mass. That's the only reason I know where he is now."

Barden considered me, then stared out the window for a moment. I felt his concern through the bond. "He's not like them. He only goes to church when he's worn and plans to go hunting. He knows he's hunting one of them and needs to be at least an even match."

Sweeping his gaze back to me, Barden eyed me for a moment, and down the bond, I felt he disagreed because the Narsitee we were hunting didn't have Vidal's morals, which automatically disadvantaged Vidal.

Instead of voicing it, Barden grunted, then grabbed his shirt and jacket. "Will you be okay while I'm gone?"

Swallowing, I nodded. "I might go down the house and study with Savas for a few hours, and then I was going to call Raisa. Between university and hunting, I've not made time to catch up with her for a few weeks, and I feel bad about that."

Barden didn't have to warn me not to go out today. Whatever happened last night spooked Vidal enough that he was scared of losing me. It was better to play it safe until we knew the threat.

"Barden, bring him home? Let's talk tonight. I don't want him thinking I don't love or want him," I pleaded.

With a grunt telling me that was his intention, Barden kissed me goodbye. Outside, he unfurled his wings and dove off the verandah.

Sighing, I grabbed my phone and texted Savas to check if he wanted to study for a while, then texted Raisa to see if we could catch up later.

SAVAS:

> Sure. But do you want to go for a flight first?
> Let off some steam so you can focus.

There was that twin bond in action again.

SASHA:

> I'll meet you in the backyard

I pressed send on my reply, just as Raisa replied.

RAISA:

> Sounds good. I'm on a sturdy date, so can
> we aim for around five tonight?

SASHA:

> A sturdy date?

RAISA:

> A STUDY date with a boy from college.
> Stupid autocorrect!

SASHA:

Is it just study?

RAISA:

Also, fun and company. We have many of the same interests and have been hanging out more, but always under the guise of studying, even if we don't get much done.

SASHA:

I can't wait to hear all about him tonight. ::wink:: I'm going to study with Savas. Msg me when you are ready.

RAISA:

K. Later.

I was happy that Raisa had someone to hang with. Not that she ever had trouble making friends, but with most of her close friends dead or having gone away for college, she worried she'd not make any new friends at university, especially when she found out that Savas and I chose to do our degrees online.

Putting my phone in my pocket, I clicked my fingers by my side to change into one of the backless athleisure wear tops I preferred for flying. Then, I grabbed my laptop and class notes and headed to the house.

A rush of adrenaline and hate traveled down the bond with Barden as my feet touched the ground. They were quickly followed by concern and disgust.

'Barden?'

Barden grunted an apology down the bond. Then shut it off. Not in the same chokehold Vidal had used. Barden's was more like shutting a soundproof window. I could still sense him and know he was okay, but I couldn't hear everything or experience the sensations he was experiencing.

It didn't upset me because he did that a lot when he was working or doing something mundane, and I did it when I needed to focus on class or being in my immediate surroundings. Barden had taught me how when we started hunting so we could shut the window enough not to distract each other, but leave it ajar so we could communicate easily still.

What Vidal did this morning was slam the window, draw the blackout blinds, and close the shutters. It was painful in its emptiness—a sensation I didn't like and had no intention of getting used to. I didn't think Vidal did either. Already, he'd lifted the shutters, and I caught glimpses of him peeking through the blinds. He'd come home tonight, and we could convince him to open the window again.

"You okay?" Savas asked from the back door, studying how I'd stopped mid-step toward the house.

Shaking off Barden's feelings, I nodded and handed over my stuff for Savas to put on the dining table. "Where are Mum and Dad?"

"Doing their taxes," Savas grumbled. We both shivered and let that thought go immediately.

Since we were five, *'Doing the taxes'* had been code for *'don't come knocking on the bedroom door'*. Initially, it was a deterrent because taxes were boring, and neither Savas nor I wanted to be stuck helping with that. Later, it worked in another way because we both figured out what it was code for and were sufficiently disgusted to never go near their wing of the house while they were *'doing the taxes'*.

Now I knew why Savas was keen on a flight. Just being in the house knowing our parents were canoodling upstairs gave us the creeps.

"So, where can we fly that keeps us out of sight and takes a good hour or more?" I asked Savas.

He smiled at me. "Why don't we take a fly in Elysia? No Vestigials there."

"True. Sounds like a plan," I agreed.

"Do you need to check in and let Barden know where you will be?" Savas asked as we headed for the garage. We'd ride our bikes the five minutes to the Gelus hall to ensure no hikers saw us.

"No. The bonus of the bond. They can find me anywhere just by thinking about me," I told Savas, ignoring the tug of pain from the missing bond. And Savas didn't need to know that Barden had shut the window. The truth was, I was probably safer in Elysia right now than here.

"Then let's go," Savas cheered.

"Race to the waterfall?" I asked, keen to burn off some of this angst already.

Savas shook his head, but his grin spread across his face. "Your mates will kill me if you come off that bike."

"Pfft! When have I ever come off my bike?"

"Which is the only reason I'm agreeing to this." Then Savas took off running, and I laughed, chasing after him.

The Narsitee

VIDAL

"DEAR GOD! YOU'RE HUGE!"

"Fuck, yes. Keep praying, baby. I love me a pious girl," I urged, threading my fingers through her chestnut hair and moving her face closer to my cock.

The little minx returned to her prayers, her hand working my length and her tongue stealing licks of my tip every time a bead of pre-cum seeped out. On her knees in her Sunday best, we were hidden by a copse of trees behind the shed at the back of the lot the church sat on.

The young thing licking my dick was making eyes at me from the moment I entered the church an hour ago, and when I had my fill of worship and left while everyone took communion, she followed me out and begged to suck my cock.

Her future was set. I looked into her eyes and perceived the good little church girl as an act. She was a wannabe cum-slut. As she'd got down on her knees and rubbed me through my pants, I'd seen her future play out. Her mind was set on her path. So much so that she openly asked me to bless her with the career and fame she so desired.

I had to say; it was the first time I'd met a girl with her heart set on being the most famous pornstar ever known. If there had been even a whisper of hesitation in her request, any static in the picture of her future, I'd have resisted, but she was driven and somehow aware of what I was. So, I'd taken her behind the hedge and obliged her desire.

Meanwhile, the final prayers of the mass were swelling my power and my dick. The Narsitee in me was in complete control right now as I watched this girl pray to my cock. I was still trying to resist the urge to lay her in the dirt and fuck her tight hole, corrupting her entirely. But I already knew that by the end of the school year, she'd have shed her innocence completely and be a party favorite amongst the senior boys. So, the god in me was okay with accepting her sacrifice in return for blessing her with the future she deeply desired.

"Lift your dress, pull down your panties, and finger your pussy," I demanded.

Without hesitation, she yanked her white lacy dress up above her boobs, pushed her panties to her knees, and slipped her finger into her cunt with a moan as she sucked my dick.

"That's it. Good girl." Controlling her head with her hair, I pushed further into that willing mouth. She choked, and her eyes teared up, but she didn't stop fingering herself or try to pull back, so I pushed to the back of her throat. "Breathe through your nose and swallow."

I waited, letting her get a feel for it, then pulled back, her drool hanging like streamers from the tip.

"You're doing well, baby cum-slut. Now suck and swallow me good."

She lunged forward and took me deep into her throat, sucking hard, keen to impress me. She certainly made up for what she lacked in skill with enthusiasm.

"God, your dick tastes so good. I want you to fuck me," she breathed between mouthfuls.

Gripping her hair, I pushed into her throat this time, my magic a torrent down my spine from her prayers.

"Vidal." Barden stepped around the edge of the hedge, his eyes widening when he saw the girl on her knees. "What the fuck?"

The girl, totally caught up in her worship of my cock, didn't even acknowledge someone else joining us. Her parents could find us right now, and she would keep deep-throating my dick and moaning for more.

"Busy," I growled, not even glancing in Barden's direction.

"Fuck, is she even legal?"

Tilting my head, I eyed the bush between her legs and the handful of boobs in her bra and shrugged. "Didn't ask. Show him your tits, sweetheart."

With her free hand, she yanked her bra cups down, her breasts spilling out, and then pinching her nipples. The move made me smile. She was going to be fun. She wasn't as young as she looked; I knew that. There was only a three-year age difference between us.

Her eyes flicked to Barden, and she fingered herself faster, sucked my cock harder. "You want him to join us? Do you want to suck his cock too?"

"Fuck off, I'm married. So are you," Barden snarled.

The girl looked back at me and pulled off my dick. "Really?" she asked excitedly. When I shrugged, she moaned. "That's so fucking hot. Please fuck me?"

Shaking my head, the smile on my face was a mix of disgust and desire. "Fucking suck me, and don't stop fingering that pussy or praying. Church is nearly finished."

No arguments. She took my dick to the back of her throat and swallowed. Closing my eyes as her internal prayers called harder to my god side, I pulled her all the way onto my dick until her lips touched my body.

"Give me a minute, brother. I'm nearly there. Yeah, that's it, little slut. Choke on it. Swallow me down."

Her mind's voice was crying 'God' over and over, and tears flowed free as her airway was shut off. But she didn't fight me. She was in thrall and would let me kill her right now if I so desired it.

"Fuck!" Letting her go, I threw her onto her back, her tits out, little white panties with daisies on them around her knees, pussy so wet it was dripping down her thighs. Fucking beautiful. Straddling her chest, I stroked my length. "Open your mouth, pretty thing."

Using her elbows to push up, she opened her mouth wide and stuck her tongue out. Growling, I gave her what she wanted, ribbons of my cum coating her mouth and tongue. Stepping back, I eyed the newborn cum-slut. She mewled and opened those legs, begging for me.

"You might want to turn around, *brother*."

"She's what, a freshman? Sophomore at best," Barden argued. "Sucking your dick is one thing, fucking her is another."

Grin getting wide, I kneeled and yanked those pretty white knickers off, then threw them at Barden. "I try to be a good guy. I do, *brother*. But sometimes, when I've reached a certain point, I must let the god in me have its way."

Cursing, Barden swept his hair back. I could feel him torn between his instinct to kill the creature ruling me right now and not being willing to hurt me. He knew I'd rather be at home with our wife curled against me watching television, but I'd reached my breaking point. I'd been denying my Narsitee nature for months, and I couldn't hold it back anymore.

"Little girl, look at me," Barden demanded, white light emanating from him as he got the girl's attention. I just laughed, already knowing that as much as the girl was in my thrall, she was a little slut and would have ridden my dick even without it. She certainly wasn't in my thrall when she first started sucking my cock.

"Do you want him to fuck you?" Barden asked the girl when he had her attention—the final hymn in the church filling the surrounding area.

Bending over, I sucked her nipple and grinned up at Barden as she arched into my mouth and yelled. "God, yes! Please fuck me. So hard. Pound my cunt. God, I want it so bad."

Lifting a brow at Barden, I laughed when he threw his hands up in dismay. "If our wife had yelled that, I would be home right now instead of here corrupting young sluts-to-be," I told him. Then slammed into that tight pussy.

The girl choked, "God!" My reward as I pounded that sweet snatch.

Forcing her to look at me, I used the thrall to rush her body to the edge, then tilted my hips on the next thrust and bathed in her climax as she shattered around my cock. "That's it, my little slut. Milk me dry. Take my cum like the good cum-slut you are."

Gritting my teeth, I came hard, pumping her full of my seed. My magic shimmered around my balls and cock, and I knew I needed to pull out—to get the fuck off this girl, but even as I told myself to back off, I smiled.

Grabbing her throat, I leaned down close, lowering my voice so Barden couldn't hear as I whispered in her ear. "You want it, don't you, pretty slut?"

"Yes," she panted.

"Tell me."

"I want your cum in every part of me. Please fill me up. I want to worship my god in every way. I want to take your seed and give you a son."

Fuck, those words did something to me. My cock hardened again, and I fucked her until we both came again.

"Church is coming out," Barden warned from the other side of the hedge.

I didn't care; I was caught up in the thrall as much as the girl. Pulling out, my cock still hard, I pushed into her tight ass. Covering the girl's mouth as she cried out. The amount of cum coating my dick eased the way as I filled her ass, then I fucked her and rubbed her clit until she came again, and I soaked her in my seed entirely.

"Thank you, God!" she panted.

Satisfied, I eased out and fixed myself up. With the Narsitee sated, the air around me snapped, giving me back my morals and capability of guilt. I looked at the mess I'd made of this girl and hated myself.

Helping her sit up, I met her eyes. "Tidy yourself up. Go to the bathroom and clean yourself up, then find your parents and be their good girl. Don't let them discover how wicked you are. It'll break their hearts."

Smirking at me with those naughty eyes, she blew me a kiss and yanked her dress down to cover herself. Stopping by Barden, she eyed him up as she took her panties back before looking back at me. "You know where to find me if you need worship again." Then she toddled off to the bathroom at the back of the church, the back of her white dress covered in dirt and my cum dripping down her legs.

Kneeling there, I hung my head. "Fuck!" I groaned at myself. Putting my head in my hands, I rocked back and forth as I cursed myself out. It was my fault I'd let it get this bad. I should have known the urge to attend church today was more than just needing a power recharge.

"Fuck!" I pounded my fists into the cum soaked ground, hating that I let it get to me. Sasha would never have loved me if she had known the type of creature I could be when I lost control. She shouldn't. I didn't deserve her or her love. She was right to reject me as her mate.

Squatting beside me, Barden put a hand on my shoulder. "Brother?"

"I promised I wouldn't be like him. I swore when I was younger, and he encouraged me to take pleasure from any cunt I desired, that I would always, always ensure I was in control. I'm not fucking in control. I'm not safe. I can't be here right now."

Barden's hand tightened on my shoulder. "If you think I would have stood by and let that happen if I knew you were just being like every other Narsitee, you are wrong. I'm a soul carrier. That girl's body may have been innocent, but her soul isn't. She loved everything that happened between you just now. She wanted it and would give you all her worship to get it."

"How did she even know that shit?" I muttered. "Girls normally call me 'god' out of habit, but that was full-on, *I know what you are, and I want to fucking worship you*' shit. From the moment she followed me out, I couldn't fight off the need to have her. I tried to sate it with the blow job, but she kept pushing my buttons."

Sighing, Barden stayed by me. "Not all souls are pure beings reincarnated. Some of those I bring over from the Vestigial hell are just as unethical as your ancestors. Worse, actually. A Narsitee does it from a place of power. They were the first beings. They created the others either through need or boredom. They've always seen their creations as their playthings. Vestigials who treat others like that are just evil."

"She's not evil. She's just... more aware than she should be."

"That girl has a soul stained in lust and narcissism, and she is still growing into her potential in this life. You are not the first man she's tried to seduce. She's been working on her pervy PE teacher for months, thinking he would be her first. That you walked into that church today, and she recognized you for what you are and desperately threw herself at your feet is not surprising. There is spiritual innocence, and then there is physical innocence. That girl only had the latter. It's why I didn't step in. You needed it, and she was willingly giving it."

Groaning, I told the absolute truth despite knowing what he was saying was true. "I knocked her up, dude."

Huffing, Barden pushed up to his full height. "If Narsitee seed took in Vestigials, they wouldn't die out. They have no women left, and human wombs are incompatible. The girl's body will reject it. The PE teacher will have fucked her by the end of this week, and she'll finger him for it if it lasts long enough to get noticed."

When I looked up at Barden, wondering how he knew that, he smirked. "I felt what you did when your other self read her. The Narsitee in you could see her future, could sense the type of girl she was; it's why you lost control of it. You normally can pull it back in line if you know you are harming. In this case, you knew you weren't harming an innocent, just awakening that girl's true nature."

Shaking my head, I shoved the guilt aside. "It won't last long enough for her to know it happened."

"Good to know." Helping me up to standing, Barden met my eyes. "Now, Simon's waiting for us, but before we meet him, I need to know exactly what your father said to you last night because you blocked Sasha and me out pretty tight."

Wincing, I brushed myself off. "I'm sorry about this morning."

Barden didn't answer.

"Is Sasha distraught?"

Grabbing my shoulders, Barden met my eyes. "She's more upset that she hurt you, that you don't want to come home because you see her hesitation as her rejecting you. She cried in my arms not because you crossed a line she didn't want to cross, but because she loves you and fears she's driven you off for good."

"Shit, I never meant for—"

"Sasha knows something went down with you last night. We felt your concern, your worry for her. She knows this morning was a result of whatever it was that happened, and so she's angry at herself for stepping into your self-destruction when she could feel it coming and intended to try and put you at ease. She's pissed at you for looking for a way to push her away instead of telling us what happened. I am, too."

"Oh, fuck off!" I shoved him away. "I would have told you and planned to tell you when I returned. You weren't there, and Sasha was running around in knickers and my jersey. She didn't even have a bra on. I tried to leave. I told her how she affected me and tried to give us some breathing room. She came down the garage naked and angry, and that's what led to that shit. I didn't intend to cause a rift there, and you know it."

Barden crossed his arms. "Tell me what your father said. Simon said whoever you spoke to last night threatened Sasha. Tell me how."

Blowing out a breath, I met his eyes. "Fine, but let's get out of here. Two men lurking behind the bushes after mass is cause for concern from the parishioners on several fronts."

Smirking, Barden gestured to the other way out, keeping us out of sight of the church. "After you."

VIDAL

"HOW'D you go at the church?" Simon asked as he showed Barden and me into his living room.

"I didn't see anyone suspicious, though the priest was a little into the service. He was shaking his booty during one of the hymns," I told Simon.

Simon frowned. "What sort of hymn can you shake your booty to?"

"They have a rock band playing the music, and they've made it all upbeat. They sing about Jesus dying for their sins like Pink wrote it." I shook my head. "Whatever keeps the youth coming to mass, I guess. The early morning mass is the more traditional piano and violin accompaniment for the old-school piety."

Shaking his head, Simon looked to Barden. "Vestigials are crazy."

Shrugging, Barden took the seat beside me. "They have their faith to explain the inexplicable. They must believe there is more to their life than kicking around for a few decades and dying."

"A lot of them just use it as a rock they can stand upon and judge others and explain away what assholes they are," I argued. "It's a form of power and control for them. But that's not why I'm still awake and sitting here."

"The threat," Simon agreed and nodded as he looked to Barden. "He fill you in?"

Barden slumped onto the sofa. "Yeah."

"I told him to step away, let those of us without a wife to lose handle it, and he drops some nonsense about the Narsitee targeting our sisters to breed their spawn," Simon complained.

Eyeing me, Barden stewed on Simon's revelation. "Sounds plausible," he finally said. "They know Vestigials can't carry to term. It makes sense that they would eventually target Orey and Gelus to see if they were more compatible."

"As if they could seduce a Gelus. Our girls could spot a Narsitee a mile out," Simon scoffed.

"Sophie didn't," I dropped straight into his silence. "And Orey girls didn't even know they existed, so my sister had no chance."

Barden grunted in agreement, then added, "I taught Sasha how to spot a predator, and yet one got close enough to her without her realizing to recognize she's mated."

"We need to work on the belief that they've gotten better at hiding from you," I told Simon.

Studying me, Barden nodded. "Or potentially, this Narsitee we are hunting is a hybrid. Maybe he blends with Vestigials just as well as we do."

How long had it taken Barden to work it out? I'd been the answer right there before him this entire time. I was still hiding that part of me from the other Gelus living here. If I could hang out with them for years and they never suspect, it makes sense another hybrid could do it too.

Simon sat back and exhaled a curse. Getting up, he swept his hand through his hair. "If that's true, he could be someone we went to school with. It would have given him the best access to the girls. Vidal here could be him."

"I didn't kill and certainly didn't fuck my sister," I snarled. "Sasha would have recognized if it were me."

Dropping his head, Simon rolled his shoulders forward. "Sorry, man. It was just hyperbole. My point remains, though, if Barden's theory is correct, this Narsitee could have been one of our classmates, come to our parties, and that's how he seduced the girls."

That made sense. Fuck knows it's what I'd been doing, though without ill intentions. "Then how do we find him?"

Simon eyed me, then Barden. "He said he's watching you."

Barden and I saw where this was heading straight away. "So, we watch who's watching you," Barden agreed.

Great. I was about to be stalked by Gelus hunters trained to find Narsitees and kill them. *'Not the best plan, brother.'*

'I've got your back,' Barden assured before returning to Simon. "I'll cover at home, though I doubt he could get past Gannix's security to get too close; it wouldn't stop him watching for you coming and going. So I can track you from the air when you are on your bike. See if anyone is regularly on your tail."

"Hawk and Falco can watch you when you work," Simon decided. "You're focused on dispatching Execrables, so it's the perfect time for him to assess your abilities and Sasha's."

"Considering our hunting grounds, that will be like finding a needle in a haystack," I argued. "You need to be watching me when I'm hunting him. He knows I am, so he's watched me do it. And I've probably come close enough to alert him, too." I turned to Barden. "You need to talk to Sasha. He's likely already interacted with her for him to get close enough to realize she's mated. See if any encounters stand out to her."

"We can ask her when we get home," Barden agreed.

Biting my tongue, I didn't refute his assumption that everything from this morning was resolved, and I'd changed my mind. I hadn't.

Letting it go, for now, we strategized how we would go about identifying this Narsitee. The problem I quickly discovered was that all those ideas could potentially expose me as well. I was going to have to get creative in how this situation unfolded.

After a few hours of planning, we said goodbye with a time and place to meet for the next hunt. As we got to our bikes, Barden eyed the long driveway. "Maybe you head out first, and I'll follow thirty seconds later. Give any tail a chance to follow you."

"I'm not coming home tonight," I finally admitted as I threw my leg over. "I'll be heading to Mum's. She's been struggling, having lost Yas, and then for me to move out almost immediately after. Jebidiah says she has empty nest syndrome and suggested I stay over now and then so she has someone to look after. Weaning her off."

It wasn't a lie, and I'd already been staying at my mum's once a week anyway when I needed time away to deal with my needs. It was easier to get to the university from my parents' place.

"If you don't come home tonight, Sasha is going to be sure you've left her," Barden worried.

Pulling on my helmet, I buckled it. "I think I should stay away at this time of the month. Let you two mate like bunnies, and I can spend time with my mum and focus on the hunt."

"Vidal—"

"What do you want from me?" I snapped. "I've abided by the rules you set down."

Noting how Barden's jaw clenched and the black channels in his eyes flared open, I knew he was reacting to the sudden gold shining out of mine.

Starting my bike, I huffed. "Tell me when it's safe to come home. I'll stay at my mother's and keep hunting this asshole." Hitting the accelerator as I kicked up the stand, I raced down the drive, leaving a pissed-off god-killer in my wake.

Down the bond, I could feel Sasha's concern for me. Honestly, I didn't deserve her. Sasha was sweet and caring, and despite how often she and Barden were fucking, she was still relatively innocent. I was pulled to her like a moth to a flame. She suffered Sophie and Yasmine's deaths as if they were her own for months on end, and she wasn't embittered by it.

I'd been so worried about her last year. She'd barely survived the incident. Then, while she struggled with her recovery, the nightmares and flashbacks should have spun her into a severe depression. Yet, Sasha dealt with it all and came out stronger on the other side. She was a fantastic creature, and she was mine. Mostly.

Ten minutes later, pulling up to the wrought iron gates of my family's home, I pressed the button to open them. Barden cruised by as the gates were wide enough for me to pass through. He gave me a nod, and then he was accelerating away again.

My phone buzzed as the gates shut behind me, and I cruised around the side of the house to the garage. Parking my bike first, I pulled my helmet off and then hit the screen to show the message where my phone sat in the cradle on my handlebars.

SASHA:

We need to talk about this morning. Please, come home.

Sighing, I stared at the message for a moment. Closing my eyes, I could envision Sasha pacing around her parents' foyer, phone in hand, chewing her thumb as she stared at the bubbles that showed I was reading her message. Closing out of the message, I watched as she saw the bubbles disappear, and no response came through. Sasha's mouth gaped open, and she typed into her phone again.

Ignoring my phone buzzing, I went through the attached garage door and left my helmet and jacket in the cubby that had always been mine in the mud room. In the space beside mine were Yasmine's school shoes and blazer, her favorite winter jacket and scarf, all still hanging, waiting for her to need them.

Touching the scarf, a memory of us waiting for our parents to be ready to go to the Tormens' two years ago, and Yas teasing me about drooling all over Sasha. It made me smile. I'd never considered how much I watched Sasha around the others. She'd been underage, and I had college girls crawling into my lap every chance they got. But Yas knew. She told me that every time Sasha smiled or laughed, I would stare at her like she was the sun, probably because it was still my favorite thing in the world.

"I can't get rid of it," Helena said softly behind me.

Dropping the end of the scarf, I turned to my mother and let her pull me into the kind of hug only a mother could give a man nearly twice her height. My mother wasn't short, but I got my height from my biological dad. Even Jebidiah only came to my shoulder.

"Don't. Every time I come home, it gives me a good memory," I muttered to my mother's head.

Squeezing me as my phone buzzed again, Helena stepped back, subtly drying her eyes as she turned to lead me into the kitchen. "I was just finishing work for the day. Give me five minutes to log out, and then I'll fix you something to eat."

"I may need your skills," I told her as I followed Helena to her home office.

"Oh?" she asked, taking the seat behind her monitors—three of them. Two were for her official work, and the third usually had a script running or a movie.

Helena had got into computers as a teen and decided that would be how she earned her money to support her Orey family. When she found herself pregnant with a Gelus in her last year of university, she chose not to return home and used some of her less legal skills in computers to supplement her income to support herself as a single mother.

Helena met Jebidiah a month before I was born and was honest that she'd gotten knocked up by a boy in college, and he'd abandoned her. Her family was strict and would not welcome a hybrid grandchild, so she chose not to go home.

Helena failed to mention that my biological father was Gelus—or at least that's what she thought–and played shocked when my wings unfurled when I was three, telling Jebidiah she had no idea her lover had been Gelus.

"We think the Narsitee who killed Yas might be blending with the Vestigials. Maybe he was a classmate of Savas and Simon's, and that's how he got close to Yasmine. He probably approached her at one of the school parties," I explained to Helena. "Any chance you can look at the records of all the guys in Savas's year and narrow our list for us?"

"I can get into the system easily, but what would I look for?" Helena pulled over a notepad and pen to jot down the details.

"Probably anything suspicious around parent involvement. High IQ, good looking, good at all the sports. Bad temper. Unusual behaviors. That sort of thing," I suggested. When Helena looked up at me, I shrugged. "Me, Mum. You're looking for someone who reminds you of me. A hybrid trying to hide in plain sight."

While my parents knew I was a hybrid, they weren't aware my father was a hybrid Narsitee. They thought he was Gelus. I'm not sure how my mum would handle knowing that the man who seduced her to bear his spawn was a demi-god and that her son was one, too.

Writing a few key things down, Helena set her pen down. "Are you staying for dinner?"

"A few days, if that's okay?"

Mum sat back in her seat. "Everything okay with you and Sasha?" Mum rarely included Barden. They knew we both married the same woman. While the Gelus just gave us interested looks and accepted it, the Orey were a little more reserved and preferred to pretend like Barden wasn't in the picture. At least, my parents did. Nash's parents just looked at us like we were circus freaks.

"Yeah, Mum. I... with hunting this thing, I can't risk it finding Sasha and—" I didn't finish that thought.

Mum's eyes teared up in understanding. I didn't want Sasha to end up like Yas. It wasn't too far from the truth. It's just that Sasha ending up dead wasn't my worst fear regarding this Narsitee.

Leaving my mum to finish up, I headed to my bedroom. It hadn't changed since I moved out, and I still had some of my clothes here, so it didn't matter I'd not brought anything with me.

Lying on my bed, I opened the messages.

SASHA:

Don't you dare leave me on read.

Vidal. Please? We need to talk about this.

You're scared by whatever happened last night, but shutting me out won't protect me. It'll just piss me off. Have you seen me when I lose my temper?

No. I didn't think anyone had ever seen Sasha lose her temper. Maybe that was what happened with Athur when he put a knife to her throat. Switching conversations, I smiled as I messaged Barden.

VIDAL:

Have you ever seen Sasha lose her temper?

It only took Barden a few seconds to respond.

And fuck, if that didn't turn me on.

The Family Dynamic

SASHA

"HE'S LEFT ME ON READ," I whispered as I stared at my phone. A tear tracked down my cheek.

"Guys do that when they aren't ready to grovel for forgiveness," Savas soothed as he stopped leaning in the doorway and came to prevent me from wearing out the tiles in the foyer. Taking my shoulders in his hands, Savas made me meet his eyes. "Girls like to talk out their feelings. Guys like to sort through them in our heads before we decide on our next move. Give him a few more hours."

"He's already had most of the day," I replied through clenched teeth.

"He was busy trying to plan the next hunt to find his sister's killer," Savas reminded me. "Now that he's got some time to himself, let him dwell in it, and you'll hear from him probably tomorrow morning."

My jaw dropped. "Tomorrow morning? I don't want to wait until tomorrow. It hurts!"

The lights in the house dimmed as if the power was about to go out, then grew brighter. Too bright.

"Sasha!" Savas snapped, bringing my attention back to him. "Count to ten."

Meeting my brother's eyes, I counted to ten; the lights returned to normal. "Sorry."

Shaking his head, Savas stepped back, taking my phone from my hands. "You're on time out until you go home." Stalking back into the dining room with my phone, Savas accepted a pat on the shoulder from my mother as he passed her.

Giving me a sympathetic look, Delila approached me, albeit warily. "That was you? The power surge?"

Chewing my lip, I couldn't meet her eyes as I raised my hand and let electricity spark across my fingers. My mother's gasp made me shut it off and drop my hand. I stood there waiting for her to be disgusted or outraged by my ability, but she just stood there quietly, pondering it.

"And your brother and father know about this." She gestured to my hand.

Inhaling through my nose, I lifted my head and rolled back my shoulders. "They found out after the Execrable attack. I used electricity, fire, and water in self-defense, so there was no hiding my ability after that. It's why Mia turned the Orey against me."

Mum did this quick head tilt with a lip quirk. "Well, it is pretty impressive and terrifying, so I can understand why she saw you as such a threat now."

"Considering the Execrable attack was set up by her to kill me in the first place, it's probably a good thing I'd always hidden my capability."

Deescalating, my mother took a step closer and caressed down my arm. "Yes. Though, I hate that you didn't feel you could trust your family with your secret."

Lifting a singular brow, I gave Delila the 'are you fucking kidding me' look she deserved. "Since my family trusted me with theirs, you mean?"

Exhaling, Delila squeezed my hand. "Your brother is right. Let Vidal sleep on whatever your fight was. His subconscious will help him process everything and see it clearer in the morning. You take after your father, wanting to make peace immediately instead of letting us simmer in our rage."

"It's not about making peace with flowery bullshit, Mum. It's about making sure that your intentions and feelings are clear. I want Vidal to know that what happened between us wasn't because I don't love him. If he knows that, we can fight about the other stuff all day."

Tears shimmered in my mother's eyes as she cupped my face and swept my hair back behind my ear. "He knows you love him, sweetheart. We sometimes forget when other things seem so significant that they're not always that important."

"Is loving someone enough?" I asked, hoping her experience and wisdom would prevail.

Licking her lips, Mum tilted her head, and a tear escaped. "Not always, no," Delila admitted. "But it will give you second and third chances to right your wrongs where a lack of love wouldn't. Your father has forgiven my temper more times than I deserve. So have you."

A tingle down my spine brought my eyes to the kitchen doorway where Barden stood in jeans and a dress shirt. Delila followed my gaze and stopped touching me as she stepped away.

"Barden," she greeted, then turned back to me.

My mother suffered Barden's presence quietly, but it was apparent her preference was Vidal. If she knew his truth, that would probably change. "I'll go help your father. Clear your study stuff and set the table, please."

Barden stepped out of the doorway to let my mum pass, then came to me. He'd showered and changed before coming down for dinner. "They're right. Give Vidal a bit of space."

Before I could respond, Barden took my face in his hands. "I know it's hurting you, but it's hurting him too. Give him time to sort through his emotions without his fear in the way."

Closing my eyes, I mentally prodded that vacancy in my stomach and winced. Opening my eyelids, I stared into Barden's black and gray striated gaze. "He told you what his father said?" I asked.

Staring into my eyes, Barden used his thumb to wipe away the singular tear that escaped. "His father carried a message from the one he hunts. They know you are mated with Vidal. He either backs off, or they'll take you from him."

"Kill me?"

"Worse. Vidal believes that whatever left you open for him to claim you as his will make you susceptible to another of his kind," Barden explained softly, keeping his voice low so that they were only for me.

I scoffed and stepped out of Barden's hands. "It won't. They can try, but the reason Vidal's bite took is the same that your kiss bound us. The bond was always there, even if I didn't realize and acknowledge it."

Titling his head like a bird hunting its prey, Barden considered me. "You seem very sure of this," he said.

Sighing, I shrugged. "I may be innocent, naive, and young in this world, but when I went flying with Savas today, I realized that this emptiness of not having him there was new, just like something was missing from my life until you came into it. It made sense then that since I've known Vidal since I was five, the bond had been there all along. This means we are soul mates or whatever connects our souls on that level of existence. They can't steal me from him without killing me, and I think I've proven enough this last year that I am not so easy to murder."

"Please." Barden glared. "Don't tempt fate. She can be a cruel mistress."

Smirking, I stepped closer until I brushed his chest and lifted my chin so he wouldn't take long to kiss me. "That's because women don't like to be mistresses. We want to be treated like we are your eternity."

Barden grunted as he wrapped his arms around me, closing all distance between us, his lips brushing mine. "You are my eternity. My everything. So don't dismiss Vidal's concern. Narsitee are not easy to fight, Sasha. Many experienced Gelus die trying."

Tracing Barden's jaw, I stared into his eyes, the concern for my well-being like a third entity between us. "I have no intention of fighting them. I need to be able to get away from it if it comes for me."

Sobering, Barden pulled back a bit. "Sash, I don't think you'll know what it is until it's on you." When I frowned, Barden caressed my face; then his hand traveled down my neck to finger the faded scar of Vidal's bite. "He's already been close enough to you to see this and know what it means. You've already come into contact with him and not realized."

Confused by that possibility, I stepped back, my hand coming to the mark. "But, how? When? I can spot Gelus a mile away now and sense Vidal."

"We think, like Vidal, this Narsitee is a hybrid who presents like a Vestigial or Orey," Barden revealed, keeping his volume low. "It's a new theory, but considering Sophie let him near her, we have to assume that, like Vidal, he's undetectable."

I stared at my husband, unable to believe that something so dangerous could be so well hidden from us. I thought of Vidal, his power, the way he kept his abilities hidden from the other Orey all these years, how even Barden didn't realize he was something else... "You can sense Gelus blood in someone. Did you sense it in Vidal?"

Barden's forehead creased as he observed me. "Yes. But it was like your mother. I knew there was some in him, but it seemed several generations removed."

"I can't sense it in any of my family, and I can only identify Gelus because of their predatory eyes. Maybe only full-blooded Gelus can pick it up, but that may help. If you come across someone who isn't Orey but has that tinge of Gelus bloodline you can sense, it might be worth considering."

Blinking at me, Barden stepped forward and caught me in a kiss that melted my bones. "You are amazing, Sash. Let me call Simon, and I'll join you for the family dinner."

Stealing another peck of his lips, I headed for the kitchen, Barden giving me a spank on the butt as he passed behind me and headed outside.

"Where is Barden going?" Dad asked.

"To call Simon. He's just had an epiphany."

"Have they made any progress on the god hunt?" Mum frowned. She'd never heard of Narsitees until Dad filled her in, and to say it made her uncomfortable to know there was what she'd termed 'a god serial killer' lurking around Canyon Falls would be underplaying my mother's reaction.

"They have. That's why Barden had to step out," I told my family but didn't elaborate. Instead, I got busy packing up my study materials and then helping set the table.

Washing my hands in the basin, I checked my reflection and smiled. Having my family together again was a relief. I was glad Mum came home. Dad and Savas needed her.

Drying my hands, I stepped out of the bathroom and ran into a man, knocking me off balance. His hands grabbed my shoulders and helped stabilize me as our eyes met. His face was without detail; only his gold eyes peered at me.

"Hello, young one. What are you doing here?" He smiled, a flash of teeth as his eyes went to my neck, and he moved closer. I shivered as his fingers caressed the bite mark on my neck, and his lips tickled my ear lobe. "You wear his mark" –he took a deep breath— "but it's not his scent you are bathed in. Normally, our kind are very territorial about our mates. It makes me wonder if you or my kin stand outside the law of chosen ones?"

The heat coming from his body was like lying in the sun in the middle of summer. It made my limbs limp, my ability to push him away gone as I struggled to fight the way he reeled me in. "Why did you kill Yasmine?" I asked.

A snicker fell from his lips, his nose dragging along my face. "I did many things with that little witch. I do like the way you Orey girls ride my dick."

The world spun, and I fell, his arms still wrapped around me until my back met something soft, his body pressing over mine. A moan sounded to the side of me, and I turned my head to see Yasmine straddling a guy on the bed next to us. I couldn't make out the man, but Yasmine was clear as she rode him hard and fast until she threw back her head and came.

Yasmine dropped beside him, panting. The guy got off the bed, yanked up his pants, and exchanged words with someone else I couldn't understand. The words were fuzzy as if I was listening through a wall. Something about a thrall. Then the other man was pulling his clothes off and climbing between Yasmine's legs, and all she did was laugh and moan as he wrapped his big hand around her throat and started fucking her.

Something about the other man made my skin crawl. I turned my gaze back to the gold eyes above me. "I wasn't the only one fucking her," he murmured in my ear. "I don't want to hurt you, young one. Tell your mate to let dead girls lie and enjoy his life."

"You killed his sister," I accused.

"She served a purpose." He paused as he lifted his gaze above me. *"Yet, she failed to be the catalyst he sought. Don't take her place."*

Everything went quiet around me. The weight above me vanished, and those gold eyes closed, leaving me in the darkness. I blinked, shadows filtered in, and something moved beside me. I jumped up and turned, ready to protect myself, only to find Barden asleep in our bed.

The clock told me it was the middle of the night, but my heart told me it wasn't just a dream. "Barden," I murmured, shaking him until he snapped awake, grabbed me, and rolled to put his body above mine while he searched the room for a threat. I had no doubt he could fill the fear building in me.

"What is it? What happened?" he whispered when he sensed the room was quiet.

"I know where I met the Narsitee for him to see Vidal's bite," I told him.

Above me, Barden stilled, his focus pinpointed on me as he listened through our bond and with his ears.

"At the graduation dinner," I gasped, remembering, breathless for some reason. "He approached me at the graduation dinner, but Vidal's mark scared him off."

The Suspects

VIDAL

SCRUBBING my hand through my hair, I opened my bedroom door and dragged my tired ass into the kitchen. My feet paused when I found Sasha sitting at the breakfast table, talking to my mother. I was momentarily annoyed that she came here to have it out, but then I noticed the pallor of her skin and how her eyes looked a little wide and cursed myself. Letting the bond open just enough to get a taste of Sasha's fear damming the other side, I was immediately wide awake.

Sasha knew I was in the room, but she didn't look at me. Instead, she picked up her mug and sipped the hot chocolate my mother made her.

Noticing me, Helena patted Sasha's hand and approached me. "She showed up half an hour ago but told me not to wake you. Talk it out, son. Please don't leave her like this. When you're done, I have results from the search you asked me to run." Mum shut the door and continued down the hall to her office.

Eyeing Sasha, who still wasn't looking at me, I sighed and set the coffee machine to run. "Let me have a coffee, then we can go to my room to talk."

"I'm not here about us," Sasha replied.

That she was here for something other than trying to mend our relationship raised my hackles. Not that it should surprise me. She loved Barden. I was always an unwanted complication in their relationship.

"The Narsitee you're hunting visited my dreams last night and spoke to me. Warned me."

Fuck. Forgetting the coffee and my previous annoyance, I moved toward my wife. She kept her head down, refusing to look at me, and it grated on my nerves. "What sort of warning?"

"He said you need to let dead girls lie and enjoy your life, that Yasmine failed to serve her purpose, and that I shouldn't take her place," Sasha conveyed. She huffed and gripped her mug tighter. "I guess he isn't aware I've already lived that death nightly for months after it happened."

What could I say to that? I knew how witnessing Yasmine's death tortured Sasha for months on end. It killed me to watch it happen and not be able to help her.

"Sasha, look at me," I demanded as I moved closer.

She didn't. Sasha kept her eyes on her mug and asked something that knocked me on my ass—figuratively. "What's the thrall?"

My jaw clenched, and I got an instant headache with the tension through my facial muscles.

"You don't want to tell me," Sasha surmised. "Have you ever used it on me?"

Fuck! "No. Absolutely not. I would never take away your will like that."

"So, it would be raping a girl to use your thrall to have sex with her?"

Did she know about the church? Is that where this line of questioning was heading?

"Not necessarily. Yes, it could be used to do that if the wielder is strong enough, but it's usually more subtle than that. It's not necessarily the Narsitee who puts someone into the thrall. Sometimes their prey falls into it from the euphoria of being in their presence while they use their power," I tried to explain. "The only time I've ever had someone get caught up in my thrall was when I was wielding my power around them. For the last person, I blessed them with the future they hoped for, and they fell into it."

"So, it's a euphoric experience for the subject?" Sasha seemed to be gathering her facts right now. I only hoped where it led wouldn't be to hating me.

"That's my experience. Yes."

"Have you ever stuck around to see the aftereffects, to see if once they wear off, they are horrified by what happened during it?"

"Did something happen when this Narsitee came to your dream last night? Did he enthrall you?" I asked, moving closer to her. I'd skin him alive if he touched Sasha like that.

"No. At least, I don't think so. I couldn't fight him off, but he didn't do anything to me; he just held me against him and whispered in my ear the entire time," Sasha revealed. She fidgeted for a moment. "He showed me Yasmine. More specifically, him and another Narsitee fucking your sister."

"Two of them?"

"Yes. The one talking to me didn't affect me, but the other one, who mentioned the thrall and had Yas after the first finished, made my skin crawl. He made me..." Sasha paused, her fingers strumming the side of the mug as she could barely sit still. Whatever she felt with this other Narsitee made her very uncomfortable.

"What, Sasha? What did he make you do?"

Finally lifting her eyes, Sasha met mine, and I saw how they were bloodshot and watery, barely holding back tears. "Return to the bridge." Silence filled the kitchen for a minute. "I don't think it was just the one Narsitee under the bridge with your sister, Vidal. I think the other one, the nasty one, got into my head and made me not see him, and I think he's the one who killed your sister."

Two of them. That would make it even harder to hunt them and keep Sasha safe. As if reading my mind, Sasha slid her chair back, stood up, and came to stand right in front of me.

"Leaving me won't protect me. It will make me more vulnerable, because the emptiness of the bond you slammed shut between us is distracting and an agony I can't ignore. Find another way to keep me safe, because this isn't acceptable."

Before I could respond, Sasha rose on her tiptoes, her hands on my pecs to steady herself, and kissed me. It was the sweetest press of lips I'd ever experienced, all innocence and vulnerability, and it made something vicious and protective flare to life inside me.

Hauling Sasha against me, I turned my head and changed our lip lock to one of pure lust and desire. Sasha moaned as her lips opened, and my tongue delved into her mouth, stroking, building the passion into an out-of-control inferno.

It was like yesterday morning in the garage all over again. Bending my knees, I gripped Sasha's tight swimmer's ass and lifted her, carrying her down the hall to my bedroom. Kicking the door shut, I told Google to play me some music, knocked up the volume on the heavy metal now playing, and dumped Sasha on my bed.

Sasha's eyes were wide as she watched me undress, her gaze latching onto my cock, saluting her, and she licked her lips. Before I could take what I'd always desired, Sasha had her hand wrapped around my base and her tongue licking and teasing the dolphin-piercing I got two years ago.

"Sasha," I groaned, my fingers threading through her hair and fisting it tight as she took me between her lips and into her throat on the first breath. "Fuck, Sash."

No matter my intentions before we left the kitchen, Sasha had seized control and was pleasuring me in a way I'd fantasized about for the last four years. Any convictions I had for why I should leave her flew out the window as she gagged and sucked and massaged my undercarriage until I was riding the edge. The bond was open; I could feel my chosen's relief and desire as she hollowed her cheeks, dragging me closer to that endpoint.

"Sasha," I warned, but it only made her work my length faster, her lips and fist meeting halfway before her tongue squiggled along my base as she drew back, the tip flicking up at the end, catching that sensitive spot every time.

Shivers raced down my spine, my balls tightened as I swelled, and then, on her next intake, I forced her down until I was deep in her throat and groaned her name in worship as she swallowed every last drop.

My head was still lifted to the ceiling when Sasha pulled off my cock, but my fingers massaged the back of her skull, making their way around until I could ease the tension in her jaw from all that sucking. Innocent my wife may have been, but she sucked cock like it was her first language.

"I love you," Sasha murmured, her voice rough and sexy. "Just because I wasn't sure how to be intimate with two men without causing jealousy or betraying one of you doesn't lessen the emotion I feel for you. It just makes me naive and vanilla. Sex is still new to me, even after a year with Barden."

A smile tugged at my lips. It was hard to take a woman's lecture seriously when she was still sitting eye to eye with my dick, let alone when she was fidgeting with my piercing.

"This was different," Sasha murmured, her ministrations slowing my shrinkage and preparing me for more. And boy, did I want so much more.

Getting to my knees, I was eye-to-eye with Sasha as I unbuttoned her jeans. "Wait until you feel it inside you," I told her.

"Do you think this is a good idea with your mum just down the hall?" Sasha asked, eyeing the door, but she lifted her sweet ass and let me yank her jeans and panties off, leaving her in just a midriff sweater.

"I'm pretty sure the music gave away what we are doing already, Sash," I told her as I massaged her thighs, using the movement to spread her legs for me. "Lie back. I want to taste you."

Not resisting, Sasha fell back on my bed, and as I lowered my mouth to her core, she combed her fingers through my hair and directed me exactly where she needed it.

My girl tasted like heaven. Ripe and juicy and super sweet. I couldn't get enough of her. Even when Sasha came all over my tongue, I craved more, making her orgasm twice more with my fingers while I lapped and sucked her clit.

After the third orgasm, Sasha curled into me for a cuddle. Sighing, I held her to me, pulled my blankets over her naked body, and kissed her crown. "I love you. I'm sorry about yesterday."

Sasha's hand over my heart tensed, and down the bond, I felt more than heard her say, "Ditto."

After thirty minutes, I slipped out of bed, dressed, and went to Helena's office.

"Has Sasha gone?" Mum asked as soon as I walked in. She removed her headphones, probably listening to her block-out-the-sex-noise playlist.

"She's asleep."

Turning to the printer, Helena grabbed a few pages and spun back on her chair to face me as she held them out. "She looked exhausted. Here are the boys who match the criteria you gave me. There weren't any in Savas's year, so I expanded the search to include the past five years at all the schools in the area. That still only gave me seven names, but I figured if he has been raised or living locally, that's where we will find him."

Taking the pages, I looked at the profiles she'd printed and flicked through them. "Thank you. I'll take these to the guys, and if any of these stand out, we can follow up."

Taking out my phone, I messaged Simon.

"Are you going to wake that poor girl up? I think she needs to sleep a bit longer," Mum lectured.

Tapping my phone against my leg, I eyed my mother.

"You could use more sleep too. Why don't you keep her company? I think it would do you both good."

That was tempting. My phone pinged, and I checked the message and replied before shoving it into my pocket. "Tell Sasha I'll be at the diner when she wakes."

The scolding glare my mother sent my way had no impact. But her words certainly packed a punch. "Your sister is going to be no less dead by waiting a few hours to soothe things over with your wife, Vidal."

"The man who killed Yas is now targeting my wife. I'm not giving him more time to plan how he can take her from me," I argued back.

Mum was on her feet instantly. "How do you know that? What happened?"

Sighing, I couldn't tell Helena that my father had visited with the warning. She didn't know I'd ever met the man or seen him regularly growing up. "That's why Sasha is so tired. The Narsitee invaded her dreams last night, showed her what he did to Yas, and warned her to make me stop hunting for him."

"They can get into your dreams?" Helena's eyes widened. "Can they hurt you that way?"

Yes. Yes, we could, but only if there had been some exchange before-hand, some way of them connecting with you biologically. All I needed was a strand of someone's hair, and I could make their dreams a prison of nightmares. This Narsitee had gotten close enough to Sash that he saw my claim, and I didn't doubt he managed to grab a stray hair from her simultaneously.

"I don't know, Mum," I lied. "You'd have to ask Barden."

Shutting her mouth on that name, Helena sat back in her chair and returned to her computer. "I'll wake Sasha at lunch if you're not back by then. Let her sleep. Hopefully she gets a few hours of peace."

I'd told Helena and Jebidiah that Sasha had been haunted by Yasmine's death, dreaming of her falling and finding her body every time she closed her eyes, adding to the trauma of already having discovered Sophie's body. My mum had always liked Sasha, so she felt terrible that Sasha was suffering.

"I'll try to be back before lunch," I told Helena. Then, I strode down the hall, collected the keys to my bike, and headed for the door.

The Study Date

SASHA

SITTING on the end of the bed, I wiped away the tears that escaped and yanked my shoes onto my feet. Ensuring I had my phone, I entered the hall and used the bathroom. I splashed cold water onto my face and then held my fingers over my eyes, hoping the cold would take down the swelling from the lack of sleep and waking up to find myself alone in Vidal's room.

He'd shut the window on our bond but left the blind open. Barden was trying to soothe me through our bond, but in a way that also let me deal with my emotions and ready for me to talk if I wanted.

Helena was in the kitchen when I went to leave. I met her eyes, so much like Yasmine's, then dropped my gaze and avoided eye contact. "I'm sorry for the noise."

"It's sweet that you blush even though you are married to him," Helena said with a chuckle. "None of the girls he used to bring home before you ever apologized, and I'd hear them over the music."

The idea of Helena hearing us humiliated me, and my entire upper body burned in humiliation for what I'd done with her son. That humored Helena even more.

"You're so young, Sasha. Most girls would be hiding the fact they have two lovers. You weren't reserved when Vidal announced your strange relationship to everyone, yet blush at the thought of someone knowing you've been intimate with them."

"My relationship with Barden and Vidal is between us, and no one outside of it gets to have a say. That doesn't give us the right to impose on others."

"So young, yet so wise. Much like my son. He's always known more than he should for his age." Helena gave me a sad smile and started fixing another cup of coffee. "He said he'd be at the Milkbar until lunch and to come and find him if you woke beforehand."

"Thank you." Heading for the door, I stopped with my hand on the handle when Helena said my name.

"Be careful, sweetheart. Losing his sister and seeing you so weak nearly broke Vidal last time. I'd hate to see what losing you would do to him."

Taking a breath, I gave Helena a false smile and stepped out, closing the door behind me. The truth is, the last twenty-four hours had given me a really good idea of what losing Vidal would do to me, and it wasn't something I was planning on experiencing permanently.

Riding up to the Milkbar, I reversed my bike into a park, then turned it off and sat there for a minute, staring across the road at nothing.

'He won't listen,' Barden's voice came over the bond. *'I wouldn't listen if you told me to stop hunting the man who killed Calliope.'*

I knew that already, but that didn't stop the idea from swirling through my brain, along with an echo of the Narsitee's voice: *'She served a purpose. Don't take her place.'*

I didn't know what that purpose was, but I was starting to think we had Yasmine's death all wrong. "I think we are getting played, and if we're not careful, we're going to play right into their hands."

'Sash—'

"Don't tell me I'm imagining things. The girl I thought was my best friend manipulated everyone around her, killed another girl out of jealousy and turned everyone against me. Mia would have gotten away with it if I hadn't touched Sophie's body at her viewing," I reminded.

The ability to see a body's last moments was still something freaky that I couldn't control, so my intention was never to touch a dead body again. Two senseless deaths were enough to experience in my lifetime.

"The only good thing about last year's nightmare was that I now know what it feels like when someone is manipulating me, and that's what this feels like—chess pieces on someone else's board."

There was a resounding silence from Barden, but I could feel his consideration of my concern, and that was enough. Throwing my leg over, I took off my helmet and headed inside the Milkbar. Vidal was nowhere to be seen, so I headed to the counter, hoping Falco or Hawk could point me in his direction. Neither of them was there, either. Some of their other staff were covering.

"Are the boys off today?" I asked the girl behind the counter. I'd never known the boys to take a weekday off.

"They called in casuals to cover last minute," she told me. "Maybe they caught that flu going around. Kitchen is still open, and food is still good though," she told me, maybe confusing my worry about the service and not that my husband was out hunting narcissistic gods.

"I don't doubt it," I told her with a half-smile. "Thanks." I turned to head home when Raisa came through the door. Her face lit up when she spotted me, and I was happy to see her.

"Sasha," Raisa greeted with a tight hug. "Are you here for lunch?"

"Was meant to be meeting Vidal, but it looks like he absconded with the brothers."

"Well, why don't you join us?" Raisa asked.

"Us?"

When Raisa pointed over her shoulder, I spotted the guy approaching the door. I swallowed my tongue when I saw the hot guy dressed in dark jeans, a heavy metal shirt, and biker boots coming through the door. It wasn't how gorgeous he was that made my throat close, but if Vidal grew out his hair and changed his look from upper-class yuppie to metal, they could be brothers. And if that didn't tell me who I was looking at, the fact that when our eyes met, the side of his mouth twitched in humor did.

"That's the guy you've been studying with?" I asked Raisa quietly.

She blushed. "I know he doesn't look like the academic type, but he's smart as anything."

I didn't doubt that for a second. When the guy sidled up to Raisa, he finally shifted his brown, human-looking eyes to my friend and cocked a brow.

Raisa rolled her eyes as she smiled up at him. "This is my best friend, Sasha. Sasha, this is Maiçon."

Offering me his hand, Maiçon grinned. "Raisa talks about you all the time."

"She does?"

"The girl with two boyfriends, right?"

Raisa's eyes widened, and she tried to elbow the guy subtly. It wouldn't have bothered me, except I knew there was an excellent reason I didn't want this guy knowing my private life any more than he already did.

"Umm." I shook my head.

"Are you joining us for lunch?" Maiçon asked, unbothered.

I didn't want to, but I also didn't want to leave Raisa alone with him. "Sure." I turned on my heel and went to the booth I'd claimed in middle school. Strange that it was always free. The only other person who ever sat here was Falco on his break. Sliding into my seat so I could see the door, Raisa slid in next to me while Maiçon stood by the table with a frown.

"What's wrong?" Raisa asked.

Maiçon pointed to a sign on the wall to my right. "It says 'reserved management'."

"Really?" I frowned, leaning towards Raisa to see what he was pointing to. "When did they put that up?"

Raisa covered her mouth as she chuckled. "It's always been there. You just seemed to miss it. Falco thought it was cute that you just claimed the spot and ignored the sign, so he let it go. No one else ever gets away with it."

Surprised by that revelation, I blinked at Raisa as Maiçon finally sat opposite us with an intrigued look. "Well, that explains why it's always free for me." I lifted a shoulder and shrugged it off with a slight embarrassment.

"What can I get you?" the waitress asked, rolling her eyes to indicate that she had heard the revelation that I had been sitting out of bounds all this time without knowing it. Falco must have told his staff to leave me be, or I'm sure they would have kicked me out by now.

We gave our orders, and then, once we were alone, I focused on the god-hybrid opposite me. "So you're a first-year like Raisa?" I asked, frowning to convey that I found that unbelievable.

The side of his mouth twitched as if he had found me subtly humorous. "In this degree, yes."

"What was your first degree?"

Maiçon didn't hesitate to answer. "Psychology. I finished honors but decided not to pursue clinical certification."

"And now you're studying Social Science?"

"I'm doing Criminology and Social Justice. It has a common first year with Raisa's degree," Maiçon answered with a smirk.

"Except he doesn't have to do the psychology subjects," Raisa complained jokingly. "But is still helping me with the assignments."

Lifting a brow, I smiled. "What will you do next year when you have no common subjects?"

"Beg and plead for Maiçon to keep helping me," Raisa laughed.

I didn't find it so funny, and when I met Maiçon's eyes, he gave me a cheeky wink and then sat back for the server to put our drinks on the table. His eyes flicked to the strawberry milkshake being set before Raisa, flashed gold, and then Raisa gasped as the server knocked it down, spilling it into her lap.

"Crap, I'm so sorry," our waitress apologized, blinking at the mess. "I'll get that cleaned up for you. I have a spare top in my bag if you need it."

"Um, I'll go see if I can clean off in the bathroom first," Raisa replied, humiliated in front of Maiçon.

Taking her hand, I murmured. "Are you okay?"

"Yeah, I'll just go clean up." Raisa wiped herself with napkins as she went to the bathroom, and the waitress wiped down the table and seat before rushing away, equally embarrassed.

Setting my glare on the Narsitee across from me, I said, "That was unnecessary."

Holding his hand in placation, Maiçon didn't look unsettled. He had that same cool composure that Vidal carried. "I needed the witch to give us a minute to talk before you decided to warn her who she was studying with."

"I'm still going to tell her."

"If you tell her my secret, I'll tell her yours," Maiçon parried.

"She already knows I'm a hybrid," I scoffed, not threatened by his warning.

"But does she know your *husband* is?" he pressed, the smirk pulling at the side of his mouth. "Does anybody know he's a hybrid? How do you think his Gelus allies would react to the news that the one helping them hunt our kind is one of us?" Maiçon watched me swallow, the joy touching both sides of his mouth now. His eyes went to my neck, and then he scooted around the curved end of the booth to sit next to me.

My pulse jumped in my throat as he caressed the tip of his finger over Vidal's claim. "Your Gelus boyfriend must be aware. Yet, he let him live and shares you with him. Why?"

Clenching my jaw, I refused to answer. Maiçon smiled in my peripheral. "Don't make me get mean to make you talk, Sasha. I don't wish you any harm. So just tell me what I want to know. Why didn't your god-killer boyfriend kill the hybrid god who claimed you from him?"

His caress of Vidal's mark turned hot, seeping into my bloodstream, relaxing me, a fog clouding my mind. "He tried. I stopped them when it hurt me. Once Barden knew Vidal's intentions, they agreed to share me."

"How? That one is not one to trust anything our kind says."

"The bond doesn't lie." Drawing strength from my bonds, I forced the fog of my mind back, clearing my head and escaping Maiçon's hold. But it didn't matter. From that little amount, he could find the rest.

"The bond? You're bonded to the Gelus as well?" Maiçon sat back, blinking at me. "You're too young to have forged a bond of exposure, so the only way you could have bonded that quickly is if you are born mates."

When I tried to slide away from him, Maiçon gripped my arm, forcing me to stay close to him. "Is that true? They are both your husbands?"

Wanting out of his hold, I put my hand to his abdomen and pushed electricity through my palm, zapping him just as effectively as a taser.

Maiçon jolted, and as soon as his hand released me, I slid away, but before I could get out of the booth, his laughter stopped me.

"Tell anyone my secret, Sasha, and I'll expose you and your Narsitee boyfriend to the locals. How accepting do you think the Gelus will be of you then? You'll be lucky if they only run you out of town."

Gritting my teeth, I turned and looked into his eyes. "Leave my friend alone, and I won't tell anyone what you really are."

"Why do you accept Vidal for who he is but assume the worst of me?" Maiçon asked. "We have the same father. We were both raised by our mothers without direct influence from him. Why can he be given your love, but I can't even be given the benefit of the doubt?"

"Vidal didn't kill an Orey girl by throwing her from the bridge," I snarled through my teeth.

Maiçon leaned forward. "Neither did I. I haven't killed a soul, and you know that. You touched me. You can read people's guilt and sins, can you not? That's how you knew your friend killed Sophie."

Talk about getting the truth from the most unlikely sources. I sat back, blinking at him. "How do you know that?"

Tilting his head, Maiçon checked around us, ensuring we still had our privacy. "Last night wasn't the first time I've visited your dreams, Sasha. I've sat through your nightmares, seen the trauma that bitch caused you. Have you told your mates that you are claustrophobic after that experience of being buried alive, or how you dream of being trapped underground again after every Execrable execution?"

I swallowed hard. I hadn't told anyone.

Sighing, Maiçon leaned toward me, his voice lowering. "I'm like my brother. I want to live and be free to do my own thing. Unlike Vidal, I didn't manage to escape our father's machinations, but I don't want to be roaming and fucking and knocking up every witch and Gelus female I can in the name of growing our numbers again. Frankly, if it would lead to more men like our father roaming the earth, I'm dead against it."

"Then why are you here? Why are you messing with Raisa?"

Maiçon's eyes were intent on mine. "I want what my brother has. I want to open myself to the potential of finding my chosen one."

"And you think Raisa could be yours?" I asked, not believing for a moment that she was.

"No. Raisa is pure Orey. I haven't so much as kissed her. My motivation for getting to know Raisa was to find a way to get close to you. I didn't think you'd recognize what I was so easily, but I should have expected that. If I had known that you generate electricity and not just pull it from the sky, I would have known better."

My mouth opened, closed, then opened again. "You think I'm your chosen one?"

Tilting his head, Maiçon flicked his eyes to the bathroom door and shuffled back to his side of the booth. "I'm not sure. I only know that you are the path to my chosen."

"And you decided now to act on that impulse?"

Shrugging his shoulder, Maiçon murmured, "Only so long can you be patient for the other party to recognize the chemistry between you. Sometimes, you must make them see what's there, light the spark, and risk the explosion."

Those words rang in my head, echoing my relationship with Vidal. "I don't know how you think I could lead you to anything except Barden's ire."

"When we finish lunch, follow me. Tell your mates you found the Narsitee and have them track you. We'll turn my father's trap back on himself."

"What trap?"

"Everyone wins out of this, Sasha. Vidal gets his sister's killer, and I find my chosen," he answered instead.

I felt that fog trying to push in again, but I forced it out. "What trap?" I pressed.

Smirking, Maiçon shook his head. "You are full of surprises, Sasha." He waited for a heartbeat, checked the bathroom direction again, and quickly said. "For a hybrid-Narsitee to fully come into their power, we have to suffer heartbreak and the grief that goes along with it. Usually, the death of someone we love and adore achieves this. My father killed my mother to hone me. Yasmine was meant to be Vidal's wake-up call."

'She served a purpose. Don't take her place'. Yasmine served a purpose and failed. She didn't affect Vidal as his father hoped because Vidal was more worried about me.

Blinking, I stood up and found Raisa standing there looking

between us. "Hey, I was just coming to check on you," I said, giving her a smile I hoped she believed, but I failed to feel.

Raisa smiled back at me and gestured to her shirt and its faint pink mark. "It might come out after a good soak, but I'll survive for today. What have you two been talking about?"

"Psychology," Maiçon replied with an easy grin.

Sucked right in, Raisa slid back into the booth, this time beside the Narsitee. Maiçon smiled at Raisa but subtly scooted aside to put some distance between them.

"Are you okay, Sash?" Raisa asked when I failed to sit back down.

"Yeah." I eased back into the booth, Maiçon's request still swirling in my head.

"Here we go." The waitress set out our meals and Raisa's replacement drink.

"You know, Sasha has to do a psychology subject as part of her degree next semester," Raisa said as they started eating.

"I'd be happy to tutor you if you need any help," Maiçon replied as expected.

"Please, Sasha was the dux of our year. She absorbs knowledge like a sponge."

The side of Maiçon's mouth kicked up in a smirk. "Doesn't surprise me. I bet you're good at sports, too. Hell, I bet you kick ass at anything you put your mind to."

"That's Sasha," Raisa chuckled. "How'd you know?"

Maiçon's eyes glinted gold as he said, "My brother is the same. You sound just like him."

"And you," Raisa added. "That describes you too."

Smiling directly at me, Maiçon said, "I guess it does."

My breath left me in a rush, my world span, and my heart raced in my chest. It couldn't be true. But the wicked glint in Maiçon's eyes told me he'd framed his words that way for a reason, and I'd caught them just as they were intended.

'If I had known that you generate electricity and not just pull it from the sky, I would have known better.'

The Bait

SASHA

"WHAT DO YOU THINK OF HIM?" Raisa asked.

With our arms linked, we watched Maiçon cross the street to his SUV. "I think that if I were still in the dating game, I'd be getting Simon Vincent to vet any potential boyfriend after what happened to Yasmine," I told her honestly.

Frowning, Raisa turned to me. "Really?"

Maiçon was in his car now. "Really. I have to go, but let's do a double date next time and see what the guys think of him. If they don't kill him five minutes after meeting him, he's probably okay," I teased and gave Raisa a smirk.

Laughing, Raisa hugged me, then headed for her car. Her parents got her the new *Model 2* as a graduation gift last year.

Seating myself on my bike, I reached down the bonds to my guys. "So, I just had lunch with a hybrid Narsitee."

The rage that blew back at me like a hot wind was expected. "We know," Barden's voice came through the Bluetooth in my helmet. "We came the moment you realized what he was."

"You screamed it at us," Vidal added.

"But other than when he put his hand on you, you didn't seem scared, so we decided to wait outside and follow when he left," Barden finished.

Checking the street, I frowned. "Where are you?"

"I'm parked out back," Vidal explained. "I was in the kitchen, ready to interfere."

Barden said, "I'm just down Waterfall Street."

Leaning to the side, I spotted Barden sitting astride his bike down the street. "Here's the plan—"

"You're going home. Barden and I will handle this," Vidal cut in.

"I'm sorry. Do you have Eyal's gift and can determine someone's guilt?" I asked.

Down the bond, Vidal tensed his jaw and clenched his fist.

"I'm following Maiçon. Vidal, you tail me and join the party once we get to the destination." I jumped in before Vidal could push back. "Barden, gather Simon and the others and give us enough time for this trap to spring."

"Trap?" Vidal asked.

"I was right earlier."

Maiçon's car door opened. His feet touched the ground, and he leaned onto his knees as he looked at me. Frowning, I removed my helmet, leaving the guys to argue why this was a bad idea. Knowing he had my attention, Maiçon crooked a finger at me and then jutted his thumb over his shoulder to indicate his passenger seat.

Swallowing, I got off my bike but didn't disconnect from the Bluetooth.

'Sasha,' Barden said my name, all his concern racing down the bond as I crossed the road out of his view and away from my bike.

"Vidal will tail me. You gather the others," I told them down the bond, then I opened the car door and climbed into his SUV, placing my helmet in the footwell. "Where are we going?"

Smirking, Maiçon pulled out onto the street. "The South Valley Pass." Then he turned on his stereo, heavy metal playing, and tapped his hands on the wheel as he navigated us out of the busy part of town.

Once we were out of town, I studied Maiçon's profile. "Are you going to hurt me?"

"I'm doing this to try and avoid you getting hurt, Sasha," Maiçon replied. He side-eyed me, then checked the rearview mirror and frowned. "You told him to come, didn't you?"

"Will you hurt him?" I parried.

"Me? No. I'm just the bait." Maiçon clenched his jaw, his fingers turning white where he gripped the wheel. "They know my brother is hunting me, so my job was to draw him in. Once we get there, I intend to protect you and ensure you escape unharmed."

"What about Vidal? What are they going to do to him?" I pressed, wanting to know I wasn't taking the man I loved to his end.

Sighing, Maiçon scratched his jaw. "There is a coming of age ceremony that all Narsitee must endure to reach their full potential. It's called enlightenment. It requires a sacrifice. Like my mother was mine, Yasmine was meant to be Vidal's."

"Except it didn't work. Yasmine wasn't the trigger you needed for Vidal."

"I told him it was a waste, that his mother would have been a better sacrifice," Maiçon said as if that was any better. "But Dad said our mothers were the wrong choice, that using my mother had created a flaw in me. Vidal has so much potential to be a powerful Narsitee that our father didn't want to make the same mistake again."

Tilting my head, I considered Maiçon. "How are you flawed?"

The side of Maiçon's mouth ticked. "It doesn't matter. The fact is, our father isn't going to give up until Vidal is enlightened."

"Am I the sacrifice?" I checked. It made sense. I was Vidal's wife; I would be the perfect way to break him.

"You would have been before he claimed you," Maiçon replied without emotion—a factual statement. "Now you are his chosen one. Killing you would likely kill him or drive him insane, and our father can't control an insane god. So, no. You are not the new sacrifice, just the" –Maiçon formed parentheses with his index fingers while keeping his palm on the wheel— "'bait' for the bait."

Maiçon turned off the main road. "Our father thinks I've used Raisa to draw you to me to bait Vidal."

"Isn't that what you have done?"

"Raisa would be in this car, too, if I'd adhered to my father's plan." Turning his head, Maiçon smiled at me. "He underestimated you; he didn't realize you'd recognize what I was on sight, let alone that you could fight off my control."

"That's what that fog on the brain feeling is?"

Cocking a brow at my question, Maiçon side-eyed me. "Is that what it feels like to you?" Focusing on the road, Maiçon indicated and pulled into a turning lane, waiting for oncoming traffic to pass. "He is coming, isn't he? I don't want to take you in if he isn't coming. You'll get hurt, Sasha, and I don't want that."

Closing my eyes, I felt down my bond.

'I'm here,' Vidal answered. *'And I've heard everything. Good job taking the helmet with you. I still don't like this plan.'*

'I'm not liking it either,' Barden added. *'I don't trust Narsitee. No matter the words coming out of his mouth.'*

'You don't have to trust him. Trust me.'

Grumbles of displeasure were my only response. Opening my eyes, I met Maiçon's gaze. "He's not far behind."

Giving me a nod, Maiçon checked the oncoming traffic and turned off the main road.

'We're turning onto the track leading to the Valley lookout, hiking track, and caves,' I informed them. "Where are you taking me?" I asked Maiçon as we headed up the gravel road.

"To a hidden gate."

"Where will it take us?" I wouldn't say I liked going through a gate without Barden. Maiçon could take me anywhere and make it hard for my husbands to find me again.

"Nowhere," Maiçon answered. "We won't be passing through." Maiçon paused for a beat. "This is a locked gate. Do you know what that means?"

"No."

"A locked gate is a pathway between two locations. Unlike the other gates, which allow you to choose your destination, this one will only carry you to one place, and only someone with Narsitee blood can open it."

That could be good or very, very bad. "And where is that?"

"This gate grants entry to our world, the realm of gods," Maiçon revealed.

Panic and fear raced down my bonds with my husbands, as well as their sudden insistence that I get out of the car now. I was not to go near that gate.

Swallowing the fear down, I fidgeted with the belt sash, wondering if I could get it off and jump from the car if needed. Indeed, I'd be better off waiting until the vehicle stopped to make a run for it. "You're taking me to the realm of gods?"

"No. As I said, we won't be passing through. Someone without Narsitee blood would die or become a thrall if they entered our realm," Maiçon said. The side of his mouth ticked up in a smirk. "As much as the idea of taking you as my pleasure slave appeals, Sasha, it wouldn't serve my purpose."

"I don't think you'd find me so easy to enthrall."

"No, I don't think you would be, but our father doesn't know that. He would think that your going through the gate would end you, and as already discussed, that would kill or drive Vidal insane. Neither one of those options is acceptable. So, you won't be passing through the gate. When we get there, I'll point it out, then I need you to stay well away from it."

"Consider it done," I assured him and my mates. I had no intention of testing my resilience to their godly powers.

Arriving at the parking lot, we left the car and, sadly, my helmet behind.

'We're taking the trail to the caves,' I told Vidal and Barden.

'I'm just at the turn-off,' Vidal informed.

Inhaling deeply, I eyed Maiçon as we headed down the trail. Glancing my way, Maiçon moved closer to me, then took my hand in his, walking as if we were boyfriend and girlfriend.

I opened my mouth to object, but Maiçon spoke first. "I'm going to need you to pretend that you're enthralled. It will justify me not bringing Raisa."

"And how would I act if I'm enthralled?" I challenged.

"It's like you're flirting with me. Lots of touching, giggling, batting your lashes, and willingness to do anything we ask," Maiçon answered factually.

"I don't think I have ever been that girl. I don't believe, even drunk with Barden naked before me, that I could ever be the sort of girl who giggles and bats their eyes."

Smirking, Maiçon squeezed my hand and stopped walking as he turned to face me. Moving quickly, he covered my mouth with his and kissed me. Two growls raged down my bonds, and then bright golden light exploded from me.

It was a flash—there and gone in a blink—but it threw Maiçon off me, landing him in the bushes behind him.

Covering my mouth, I laughed, but only from the sheer surprise of that happening.

In a blink, Maiçon was in front of me again; my face braced in his hands as he stared into my eyes, his pupils liquid gold as he growled right back at my mates. "Fuck you! I'm not playing games. I'm trying to protect her and make sure she comes home to you. If you don't want me to touch her, you do it. I dare you to show your mate what you can do to an unsuspecting witch. Even you aren't innocent, god-killer. The Gelus are master seducers. I've been in her dreams; I witnessed that stunt you pulled in the hallway when you wanted to make sure she chose you and not any of the witches."

The snarls down the bond petted out. Maiçon stared into my eyes with his liquid gold gaze, and as my mates fell back into silence, the side of Maiçon's mouth twitched. "That's what I thought. Neither of you is willing to show her your dark side."

Maiçon lowered his mouth to mine again, but just before our lips touched, the sound of someone approaching on hurried, angry steps broke us apart. As we turned, Vidal was storming down the trail. He raised his helmet and threw it hard at his brother, Maiçon catching it with a grunt to the gut.

Before I could react, Vidal had me in his arms, his eyes molten gold as he kissed me. Our bond opened wide, his heat poured into me, and I lifted on my tiptoes to get closer, our mouths feeding at each other as if we'd been starving and we were each other's craving.

My back hit a tree, my legs wrapped around Vidal, and he became my everything. The world outside of us and our bond didn't exist as I lost myself in him, how good he felt, and how perfect just touching him made me. It was a euphoric, out-of-body, out-of-mind experience. I was just floating in his light, basking in the essence of a god. I would do anything to stay here, give him anything if he made me feel like this forever.

My mind snapped back as if it was elastic and had stretched too far. I jolted, but firm hands held me securely. Closing out the kiss, Vidal stared into my eyes. "You pulled yourself out of it," he whispered, sounding awed. "I would have pulled you back gently, but you freed yourself. How?"

Swallowing, I didn't dare try to use my words. *'Not now, it's not safe. I'll explain my theory later.'*

Caressing my face, Vidal watched me a moment longer. "What you just felt, that euphoria, that's the thrall. Imagine he made you feel like that and hold that sensation. The others will believe you are enthralled." Stepping back, Vidal watched me a moment later, then turned to his brother. "If you hurt her, if you betray us, or if you try to seduce her again, I'll tear you apart."

Tossing Vidal his helmet back, Maiçon smirked. "Nice to finally meet you, little brother. Don't you worry; I won't let anything harm her." He offered me his hand, and when I took it, Maiçon gave Vidal a wink and led me down the track.

As we approached the mouth of the cave, I glanced over my shoulder; Vidal wasn't there. Frowning, I peered up at Maiçon, worried I was losing my mind.

'I'm here,' Vidal assured, his presence radiating down the bond, giving me a touch of that euphoria again.

Knowing he was right there with me, I gave Maiçon the smile I wanted to give to the man I loved. Maiçon noticed, snickered to himself, and shook his head. "I can't wait to know what that feels like."

Then we were shadowed by the cave opening, and the darkness beckoned us to join it.

The Ambush

VIDAL

"I DON'T LIKE THIS," I snapped.

'You've mentioned already,' Barden snapped back. *'Trust our wife.'*

"I trust Sasha implicitly. I don't trust anyone else with her. Especially not one of them."

'Nice to finally meet you, little brother.'

Did I have a brother? All these years, my father had never mentioned another son, never told me about a brother, let alone let me meet him, and now that brother had my chosen one in a cave with a one-way gate to the realm of gods—a gate that would kill her instantly if he took her through it.

'I don't trust him either, but I know Sasha and what she is capable of.' When Barden's voice came down the bond next, it was low and quiet. *'She is a god's chosen one. That isn't a weakness, Vidal, it's a fucking forcefield.'*

Barden was right. From the moment I bit Sasha, the bond that drew us together banded around us, tying us together but protecting us. That moment of intimacy we'd shared this morning had only reinforced the bond. If we joined our bodies like nature intended, it would become impenetrable. I knew this; I could feel it in my bones as if it were second nature.

Sick of waiting, I left my spot on one of the boulders outside the cave's mouth. 'I'm going in,' I said.

'We're turning off the highway,' Barden informed.

Only ten meters into the cave system, it branched off to two paths. I wasn't sure which route to take, but then a warm breeze came from the right, carrying the scent of air disturbed by lightning during a rainstorm. I didn't even realize Sasha smelled like a thunderstorm until this moment. Yet, as that breeze tickled my flesh, I recognized Sasha behind it.

Moving into that arm, I followed that tickle of air from branch to branch, going deeper and deeper into the caves. Eventually, I came to a side tunnel signposted for experienced spelunkers only. Fear and panic were pulsing down the strong bond.

'Sasha is claustrophobic,' I acknowledged to Barden.

'She was buried alive. I'm surprised she could push past this fear even to enter the cave.'

'I doubt she expected it to be so deep, possibly thought it would be like the veil and just inside the opening,' I theorized.

'How deep are you?'

'I've been in here for twenty minutes and reached the point where the signs strongly suggest I not go any further.'

'We've just reached the mouth of the cave; give me a path so I can find you quickly.'

Looking over my shoulder, I felt the earth beneath my feet, then raised my hand to waist height. As I did, a trail of exposed amethyst bloomed along the bottom of the wall, returning to the opening. Bending to touch the closest jagged crystal, I pricked my finger to draw blood. The crystal darkened and lit up as if on LED lighting, racing back into the cavern.

'Neat trick,' Barden chuckled.

Ignoring his snark, I traveled into the tighter passage and understood why Sasha was bordering on having a full-on panic attack. How she was meant to feign being under the thrall when her anxiety was this high, I didn't know, and I doubted she could. I had to shuffle sideways with my knees bent to get through tight spaces.

After a few minutes, I emerged into a large chamber full of light. At first, I thought there was a well, but as I scanned the space, I realized the light came from a water pool and the algae covering the bottom and sides. A minor aquifer ran through the cavern halfway up one wall, falling into the pond and then out under a far wall. I could sit here for hours and admire the beauty of this place, but the rising panic of my chosen one had me skimming the small path around the edge and the corner into an attached smaller space, which was also a dead end.

I found my chosen one in the arms of the brother I never knew. If they'd been kissing, I'd have been jealous and probably launched myself at him. Then again, we'd have felt that down the bond and forced him back before he could put his lips on her. Instead, this Narsitee was hugging Sasha, rubbing her back, her face buried in his chest, and her eyes closed. It looked intimate, but the bond told me his hold was the only reason Sasha wasn't running for the exit.

"Sasha," I murmured, the space-carrying sound quite well.

Pulling away from the Narsitee, Sasha stepped towards me, but he caught her wrist and said, "Stay by me."

Looking over her shoulder, it took Sasha a second, but slowly, she smiled up at him and stepped back to have her back to his front. The Narsitee wrapped an arm around her, locking her into his hold, then lowered his mouth to her ear and whispered something.

Despite the anxiety pumping down the bond from Sash, she leaned into him and closed her eyes in a happy sigh, playing the part of enthralled beautifully.

The Narsitee peered at me with narrowed golden eyes as he started kissing down my wife's neck.

"Get the fuck away from her," I snapped, ready to charge him.

Ignoring me, he stroked Sasha's collarbone with his tongue. He chuckled when Sasha shifted her weight, subtly shoving him back with her butt. It looked like she was turned on, but down the bond, I could tell that wasn't the case.

"You fuc—" I lunged for him only to slam into a glass wall.

"Temper, temper, brother," the asshole said with a chuckle. "I was an only child, and I know how to share better than you."

Sasha lifted her head slightly, her eyes opening a crack, but the Narsitee cupped her face and pressed his lips to hers.

Blinking, I realized the bond was closed. This son of a narcissistic god had done to me exactly what I did to Barden the day I claimed my chosen. Slamming against the glass between us, I tried to force the bond open. "Let her go; this is between you and me."

Ignoring me, the Narsitee kept kissing my wife. Sasha was tense, but she was also kissing him back. She didn't know what was happening, but I did. I knew what this bastard was about to do. "Sasha, don't trust him. He's smothered our bond. Come on, baby, come back to me."

Sasha pulled back and looked from him to me, but before she could remove herself from the situation, the Narsitee whispered to her again, and then they were kissing again.

'Barden, help me open the bond. This son of a bitch is going to—'

Before I could finish the warning, the Narsitee struck. He dropped his mouth to Sasha's neck and bit her.

"No! Stop."

The lying piece of shit met my gaze, his swirling molten gold. Static filled my head, and then, as a distant thought, I heard him. *'I'm saving her life.'*

"I warned you." A new voice joined me—a voice I knew. The shadow came from the dark, curved wall section; without even thinking about it, I knew it was the gate. As promised, my brother had Sasha as far from it as he could in this small cavern, and now that my father had emerged, he'd shifted Sasha subtly to be on his other side, putting his body between her and her doom.

Turning on my father, I gritted my teeth. "And you let him. She's my chosen one. There is an understanding—"

My father's face turned vicious as he got right up in my personal space. "An understanding you were denied when you turned on your kind and started hunting us with them," Linus spat as he gestured angrily to Sasha.

My brother had finished making his claim and supported Sasha as she hid her face against his chest, clinging to him. She looked pale, her body trembling.

Curling my fingers into my palm, I tensed my fists as I pointed angrily at the one who had my chosen. "He killed my sister," I snapped back at Linus.

"No, he didn't," Sasha voiced, then choked off suddenly. Her eyes went wide as she stared up at the Narsitee holding her. His eyes glared over her head at my father.

I blinked. Was he angry at my father for silencing Sasha's defense of him?

Linus moved over to stand by his other son, revealing that the wall between us was gone. I hadn't made my move yet. Sasha had warned me it was a trap, and we needed to spring it first.

Linus eyed Sasha like a piece of meat and licked his lips. Fucking gross! He wanted to fuck my chosen.

"Your sister was a valuable loss. It was unfortunate, but Maiçon didn't know that you loved another more, or she would still be alive."

'He lies!' Sasha's voice echoed down the bond, a distance between us that wasn't usually there, but the bond was still strong. *'I can read Maiçon's guilt, and none of it is related to the death of an innocent.'*

'He is a Narsitee. They don't feel guilt,' Barden and I schooled her simultaneously.

'Eyal's gift isn't confused by Narcissism,' Sasha defended. *'This isn't Yasmine's killer. We wouldn't be standing here if he was, I would never have entered this fucking death trap.'*

Sasha's eyes raked the earthen ceiling of the cavern and trembled harder. Focusing on my father's words, I watched him reach and caress her pale cheek with gritted teeth. I wanted to turn him inside out just for that one touch, for even thinking lewdly about her.

Sasha jolted, her eyes growing glassy as he touched her. Panic, fear, and trauma all too familiar from her experience of witnessing my sister's death echoed down the bond. Not that my father seemed to notice the shift in Sasha's demeanor. She wasn't trying to pretend to be enthralled anymore.

"She is beautiful," Linus complimented. "But now that you are bonded, she's useless to me, just as your sister turned out to be." Sighing, he dropped his hand and moved back to the far corner, leaving Sasha staring after him with wide, tear-filled eyes.

'It was him.'

"For a Narsitee hybrid to come into their full God powers, he has to experience absolute heartbreak or suffer absolute betrayal. There is only one way I can give you your power now, son. I'm sorry."

'Vidal, it was him.'

"It's time," Linus said as he reached the corner and yanked another person I hadn't seen there to their feet.

'Vidal, your father killed Yasmine.'

I registered Sasha's words somewhere when I recognized the woman being dragged towards me was my mother.

"Vidal," Helena screamed for me as Linus dragged her towards the gate. The Gelus stormed into the cavern, glowing swords in hand.

"What are you doing?" I moved to intercept them but lost my father's attention as Sasha had already seen what he intended and moved.

Slamming into my father, I expected Sasha to try to tackle him. Instead, she suddenly glowed with electricity and sent Linus flying into the opposite wall, a branch of lightning following him across the cavern.

Maiçon and I were both moving to reach Sasha and my mother as my father flung out his hand. I managed to snag my mother's forearm and yank her aside as my brother and I went for Sasha—too late. Her body jolted like she'd been impaled, blood coughed from her lips, and she stumbled.

"No!" I screamed as Maiçon did, and then Sasha fell through the dark earthen wall that was the gate to a forbidden realm. Pain ripped down the bond, and then there was nothing. I cried out, "Sasha!" hoping it would pull her back to me. I had to go after her.

I turned to let Barden know I would return her just in time to see my father look toward my mother. I shifted to get in the way. There was a yell. Golden wings—too gold to be mine—wrapped around Helena and me for just a moment, and then, as I glanced to the side, my brother met my eyes.

"I'm sorry. I failed you," he whispered. Blood spat from his lips as he fell back. I reached for him, but he swung his arm away and fell into the gate, disappearing as my wife had.

A growling came from behind me. Barden, enraged, fighting my father, his sword glowing like the sun. My father's sword was dark steel that glowed gold and red around the edges, like a solar eclipse.

"Get my mother out of here," I yelled to Simon and the brothers.

"Sasha," Falco worried.

Ignoring him, I stormed towards my father, my power filling my veins, lightning branching down my spine and across my ribs. My brown-gold wings exploded from my back, glowing golden in the din. Grabbing Barden by the back of his jeans, I yanked him back and threw him towards the door with barely effort. *'He's mine to kill, brother,'* I warned as I squared off to face my father.

"What the fuck? He's a hybrid?" Hawk asked as he helped Barden up. Barden was struggling to get his feet under him.

Linus blinked wide eyes at me as he withdrew. "What... how?"

"Last year, I watched my chosen one marry her Gelus mate. The heartache of losing her without ever having the chance to claim her finalized my coming of age," I raged at my father. "The same day you threw my sister to her death from the underpass. An action that then killed my mate."

Showing my teeth, I reached deep into the earth, further than my Gelus powers alone would have allowed. Not only did I carry the Narsitee power, but those powers amplified those of my Gelus genes.

"Your actions were wasteful. I was awakening to my powers while my mate fought for her life. It was the delicate tethers of the potential bond I held with her that saved her. I used my awakening to save her before I lost consciousness." I tilted my head to appraise my father. "You did this to make me your son, but you failed—because I may be your blood, but I am not heartless like you."

The ground trembled, and then giant spears of amethyst ejected from the walls and floor of the cave around Linus, impaling him several times.

Bloody and still in shock, Linus stared at me, mouth open. For a moment, I felt the call to let it all go, to destroy everything and everyone in the grief of losing my mate, but then a soft brush over my shoulder pulled me back from the edge of insanity.

Barden stood there, hand there, reminding me I wasn't alone in my grief. We exchanged a knowing glance; his black orbs rouletted with gray, reflecting my golden flame irises. Barden nodded once, stepped forward, swung his sun sword, and my father's head flew up.

I marveled how the head turned to ash as it reached the trajectory of its upward spin, then it disintegrated and fell with the ashes of his body to the cavern floor.

When Barden turned to face me, I met his eyes and said, "Get my mother home. I'm going for our wife." In two steps, I was falling through the gate.

The Narsitee

SASHA

PAIN RADIATED through my body as I stumbled out of the darkness and onto the precipice of the cliff edge. My eyes widened, my arms windmilled to prevent my forward momentum as I stared at the nothingness beyond. No, not nothingness, clouds. We were so far up on a mountain that the clouds blocked the view of what was beneath us.

I gasped in another breath as more pain shot from my core. This was like a zipper closing, knitting together the flesh Vidal's dad had sliced open. My back arched with agony, and I started to fall back toward the gate, paralyzed by it; then, something impacted me from behind, and I was hurtling forward and over the edge.

"Sasha," a pained moan called behind me, distant from the wind tearing past me as I fell into the clouds. A flash of golden wings followed me over the edge.

Moisture licked my skin and clothes, and the clouds coated me and left me saturated. This was why Barden and Savas told me to stay out of the clouds. My wings still worked when wet, but not when drenched.

'There are air pockets in the clouds, but you can't fly in the water, Sasha, and the clouds are like deep puddles on a pitted road—more water than air,' Barden warned in those early days of learning to fly.

So, I didn't try to save myself. I just closed my eyes and fell into whatever my fate was now.

An arm swept around my waist, the large hand covering my lower back as it jerked and pulled me tight to the rigid body it belonged to. "Sasha, I'm so sorry."

Opening my eyes, I stared up into Vidal's brother's guilt-ridden golden gaze. Blood smeared his chin, agony and rain covered his handsome features, his brown hair darker drenched. He looked like he had emerged from a shower, and I guessed I must have looked much the same.

"I'm sorry," he whispered again, as if everything that happened was his fault, as if he'd betrayed us instead of trying to save us.

With one arm wrapped around his neck, I caressed his face, my thumb wiping the blood from his chin, letting him know by touch there was nothing to forgive. Then, wrapping myself into him, I caressed the top of his wing, the feathers water-logged.

"Your wings," I whispered in his ear, tears leaking from my eyes as I realized they were dead weights on his back in this state.

His large palms pressed into the center of my back, and Maiçon held me tighter. "The fall won't kill us," he muttered.

"Only the landing," I added.

Maiçon snorted into my neck. "I knew I liked you for a reason."

Sunlight suddenly warmed my cold, wet body. Opening my eyes, I saw that we'd left the clouds and were falling through the open air. Grunting, Maiçon spread his wings, not to fly but to slow down our trajectory and try to dry the feathers out.

Glancing over my shoulder, I finally saw the ground. Beautiful turquoise interspersed between jagged spheres of rock pillars.

"Oh god!" Tingles raced up my spine.

"Say that again," Maiçon demanded.

"Do we have time?"

"Buy us time. Pray to me!"

I did. I prayed to this god, to any god, to all the gods to somehow pull our survival out of the bag because if we didn't spear ourselves on the tip of one of those pointy pillars or smash into the jagged edges of their sides, we were going to smash into the deep waters around the base of them.

So, I prayed, and as the first spear of rock appeared in my periphery, I prayed harder. "Oh, god, god, god, god, god, fuck, god, fuck, fuck, fuck, Maiçon!" I screamed as another pillar came up on our other side, so close Maiçon had to adjust his wings to avoid the collision.

"Fuck, Sasha, keep praying, close your eyes, and don't stop praying, no matter what. Keep calling to me, and don't let me go," Maiçon yelled, then he threw his weight to the side. I screamed as we impacted, Maiçon taking the hit and the force of it reverberating through my body, winding me. I nearly lost my grip on him, but Maiçon tensed his arms with a curse as we rebounded off that first hit and fell, only for Maiçon to impact, bounce, impact, drag, drop, hit, be thrown into the air again, and keep falling.

In my head, I kept praying to him, for him, for us. With every impact, grunt, or curse that left Maiçon's lips, I prayed harder and with firm intent that we could survive this. That this wouldn't kill us, that somehow, we'd live to see another day.

The next hit, Maiçon didn't make any noise, his hands loosened, then let go altogether as his body went limp.

"Maiçon," I screamed as we rolled free from this ledge and fell again. "God, Maiçon, please!" I begged and pleaded, clinging to him as he became the weight that pulled me over the edge and finally into the raging waters that would likely become our graves.

I clung to Maiçon, even as he acted as an anchor as the darkness closed over us, but I wasn't scared, not here, not in an element that was as familiar to me as the blood in my veins. Closing my eyes, I sent tendrils of my powers into the water, the current already stealing us away. I wrapped a cocoon of protection around us, using the water-like wrappings of bubble wrap to keep us from slamming into the pillars and holding us together.

'Take us to safety,' I demanded. Then I closed my eyes and prayed to Maiçon that he would be okay.

We were expelled from the currents and forced upwards at speed, waking me from the darkness I'd fallen into. Maiçon was still unresponsive and still in my hold as we breached the surface, and I sucked in a deep lungful of air. How we'd survived without it beneath the surface, I didn't know, and I wasn't going to stop and calculate why I was even alive right now.

Familiar tingles raced down my spine, making me smile. "Vidal."

I got only an answering tug down our bond in reply, but it eased my mind as the waves picked us up and rushed Maiçon to shore. Luckily, I'd always been a strong swimmer, and I could keep one arm around Maiçon's chest while using the other to swim us in until we were in the knee-deep waters of a beach.

Dragging Maiçon's body as far out of the water as I could, I eventually gave out when only his legs were still submerged. Collapsing down beside him, I panted for breath for a moment.

"Shit," I muttered to myself as my eyes landed on one of Maiçon's wings; it was bloody and mangled. "Oh, god." I reached over Maiçon to see the other wing, which was in even worse condition. It looked like the fall had tried to rip them from his back.

Tears fell as I draped one of his arms over his body and bent up one of his knees, using the leverage to roll him into the recovery position.

A gasp left my lips at the state of Maiçon's back, my hand going to my mouth when I saw the back of his head and understood what had finally made him lose his hold on me. "Oh, god, Maiçon," I whispered. Leaning forward hesitantly, terrified of Eyal's gift traumatizing me with experiencing Maiçon's fall as if it was mine, I put my fingers to his neck, hoping to find some sign he could survive these injuries.

There was no pulse. Still, Maiçon only looked to be sleeping, not dead like Sophie and Yasmine had. He had more color, and as my hand lingered, I noted his body was still warm, despite the cold we'd just spent God knew how long in.

Most surprising was that my gift wasn't activating or giving me anything.

"It only works on mortals," a man's voice answered my unasked question, making me jump back and cringe at the pain in my hands.

Pulling them before me, I noticed the bruising and grazes over the backs of my hands and forearms. I'd had them around Maiçon, yet I hadn't registered that my arms had been between his body and the rock every time his back hit a pillar.

The man standing a few meters away cocked his head as he continued talking, his eyes never leaving me. "Or the long-lived creatures of Elysia like your kin."

"Who are you?" I asked, trembling at the awareness of his power. I was pretty sure the man standing with the sun to his back so that I couldn't make out his features was not a hybrid of any sort. Which only left one type of being, if Maiçon had told me the truth about which realm that gate led to.

The sides of his mouth seemed to tilt up, and then he squatted to eye level, revealing his face to me. "Grandpa?" I gasped. It was like looking at my mother's father or my great-uncle Billeizum, whom Nelly introduced me to.

The Narsitee smirked. "I am probably several generations removed, but my genes have always been strong, and the men of my line bear a striking resemblance." He tilted his head to study me. "You are one of Eyal's line, I see. My son's gift always throws a certain air around it."

"Eyal was a demi-god?" I asked, my voice breathy with awe and fear.

The Narsitee smiled as he mouthed the word, 'god,' but didn't confirm. "It was that name that drew me to you. When you call for power and help in this realm, it calls to your closest kin, not the one closest to you. Which is a good thing, considering in whose abode you dragged yourself ashore."

Rising to his full height, he ignored Maiçon and came around him to me. "Can you help him?" I asked, jumping up to my feet and gesturing back to the body on the beach while taking a few steps back so he couldn't touch me.

Stopping his advance, the Narsitee's smile dimmed. "He doesn't want my help. No one with any sense about them would." Lifting his hand as if he would touch me, the Narsitee paused, tilted his head the other way, and frowned. "You don't know."

"Know what?"

"Who I am, from whom your blood origins come, and why you can see a mortal's death?" Still holding his hand ready to reach me, the

Narsitee waited another second. Lightning flashed behind my eyes, the sky turned dark, the wind howled, and a figure in a long black hooded robe stood before me as his enormous black wings unfurled behind him.

His gloved hand slipped around the back of my neck and hauled me against him. His hood hid the beauty of his face, leaving me staring into a galaxy of constellations. A lifetime of teachings fell from his lips in another language without a sound, yet somehow, I understood every utterance.

When it was done, he relaxed his hold on me, letting me draw back. He kissed my forehead and said, "You need to wake up, my child."

I jolted awake, sitting up where I lay with an arm around Maiçon, his face tucked into my chest. He was still warm, not cold, despite the sun having set. Blinking, I took in the blanket that covered our lower bodies, another under us. There was a nice fire burning in a pit dug into the sand beside us, bottles of water, and a platter of food waiting to be consumed.

Frowning, I got to my feet and moved out of the firelight to take in my surroundings. We were still on the beach but far away from the water and weren't alone. "Vidal," I breathed.

I was running toward him as he turned to my call. He only took two steps toward me before I was in his arms, hugging him tight and kissing his cheek, jaw, neck, and eyes.

"Fuck, Sash, you scared the shit out of me," he choked as he held me just as tightly.

"When did you find me? Why are we still here?"

"Before the sun descended. You wouldn't stir when I tried to wake you, and he—" Vidal looked toward the fire and his brother's body and swallowed whatever he planned to say. He didn't have to. Our bond was alive and as open as it could get.

"I healed him, but the damage done to his head—" Vidal broke off again, shook his head, and exhaled. "He'll need to sleep it off, and we can't take him home until he does. This realm is the source of all life and all power. It gives that power to its children freely. Right now, being here is the only reason he's alive."

"You can heal?"

"All Narsitee can heal, but only specific Narsitee can bring someone back from the brink of death." Vidal studied me, a question I probably didn't want to answer but wouldn't be able to hide the truth of the answer. "You're still alive and not enthralled," Vidal stated instead of asking.

"I am," I confirmed the unasked. We were silent, studying one another for a moment.

Vidal cupped my cheek, traced my lower lip with his thumb, and murmured, "I'm relieved." Urging me closer, he kissed me.

So much love passed between us in that one lock of lips. It was slow, emotional, and tender as we both lingered in that moment of connection again. Vidal pulled me closer; I crushed myself against his front, my hands hooked over his shoulders to make sure there was not a breath of space between us.

As that first kiss closed out, Vidal tilted his head, and all the longing took over. When he squeezed my ass and lifted me, I wrapped my legs around him tight, panting into his mouth between passionate kisses so hot they made the fire we were walking towards feel cold.

Stopping by a nest of blankets on the far side of the pit from Maiçon, Vidal lowered me to my feet, then cupped my face. "Tell me you want this, Sasha."

"I want this," I assured, stepping close to him, my hands rubbing across his toned chest, to his shoulders, then back down, brushing over his nipples and to his jeans. I unbuttoned the fly as I confessed, "I need you."

Vidal's mouth crashed over mine, our hands frantic as we divested each other of our clothing. We fell into the nest of blankets, entangled in each other, touching and caressing, kissing, licking, and sucking on every inch of skin we could reach.

My fingers threaded into Vidal's hair as he kissed between my thighs, making me call his name to the sky as he took me to heaven. Every sip, lick, and suck of his mouth was... godly. When my back arched and I came on his tongue, I floated in the stars. It was an authentic out-of-body experience.

Crawling back up my body, Vidal stared down at me with his milk chocolate eyes, awe in his features. "Sasha," he whispered my name in pure reverence. "My goddess."

Tingles of power cracked down my spine, lightning branching down my nerves. It was a fantastic feeling—heady and addictive.

Then Vidal was pushing into me, filling me up, finalizing our bond, tethering us in the physical so that it was no longer intangible. He paused when he was as deep as he could go and stared down at me. Vidal smiled at me with pure adoration, sweeping my hair back from my face. "I'd given up hope of ever getting to love you like this. Thank you for not giving up on me, for loving me."

Before I could respond, Vidal's mouth silenced me, and then his body moved with mine. Vidal took me slow, grinding and winding his hips as he moved in and out of me, driving me quickly to the precipice again.

My body tightened when my fingers clenched on his biceps, and I breathed his name; Vidal used the arch of my back to sweep an arm under me, lift me, and flip us.

Pulling my knees up, I straddled him, winding my hips, using my hands on his upper chest to work our bodies closer to the precipice, taking him even deeper until the orgasm building switched from the G to the cervix.

"Vidal," I called out his name as that more intense climax started to escalate.

Using his defined abs to crunch up, Vidal cupped my cheek to guide my lips to his, and his other hand pressed into the curve of my spine, arching me, forcing me to take him deeper. He dropped his mouth to my nipple, my core spasmed, and from one pinch of his lips to the next, we moved from making love to fast and hard fucking.

Gripping his shoulders, I cried his name as my body disintegrated into euphoria; the dangerous sensation of the thrall swept over me as Vidal yelled my name and claimed me as his, and then he held me to him tightly, both of us breathing hard as we lingered in the bliss.

Slowly, I came back to myself in his arms. We were lying, a blanket over us, his cock still inside me as we recovered.

"How did you get the blankets and food?"

"This realm is power, and we are limitless in using that power."

Sighing, I accepted that it made sense. "How come you can heal and I can't?"

Caressing my spine, Vidal kissed my shoulder. "You haven't been fully awakened into your Narsitee powers."

"It's done by experiencing great betrayal or grief, right?" I asked, thinking back to last year.

"Apparently."

"And I caused you to go through it?"

Kissing to my ear, Vidal nibbled. "It's not a bad thing to experience, Sash. It's like getting the most amazing head you'll ever have, all this power coursing into you, filling you to the brim, and begging you to use it. For most Narsitee, the triggering experience makes it easy to use that power for something bad, and once you do, you can't turn back from it."

"That's what your father wanted with you? Maiçon said your father told him that using his mother as his trigger messed up the process and that Maiçon was a failure. That's why he didn't want to use Helena to trigger you," I revealed.

"Maybe. It didn't work. You triggered me, but all I ever wanted was your happiness, Sasha, so I couldn't hate you for choosing him. Then a few hours later, while I was lying experiencing..." Vidal looked confused, as if finding the right word was hard.

"The best head you'd ever had?" I teased.

He smiled. "Yes. I felt this secondary grief, this snapping of tiny threads, and realized it was our unfulfilled bond. At first, I thought it was because you wed Barden, but the pain, the nothingness, made me panic. My love for you caused me to direct that power down our bond, and when I did, I realized you were dying."

"It's why you couldn't resist biting me the day you came for my secrets, right? Saving me that day strengthened the bond, and it wouldn't be refused."

Caressing my neck, Vidal stared into my eyes. "I couldn't resist you because I love you. The bond was just an invisible force urging us. My love for you wouldn't let me deny our connection any longer."

"I love you too," I whispered.

Drawing me closer, Vidal whispered back, "I know." Then his lips pinched mine, and we lost ourselves physically exploring our emotions.

The New Secret

VIDAL

SASHA WAS asleep in my arms when movement on the other side of the fire caught my attention. Dawn was fast approaching, and the sky was already starting to lighten. Shifting carefully so I didn't wake my wife, I slipped from beneath the blankets and yanked on my jeans. I shook out her clothes and bundled them under the blanket so they'd be warm for her and easy to reach. Then, I moved to the other side and dropped beside my brother.

In silence, he handed me the platter of food he'd been nibbling from. "You lied to her about the awakening."

Glaring at the guy who could be my twin, I shook my head. "She found out her friend purposefully buried her alive, and at the same time, she discovered her family had been lying to her about who she was her entire life. I didn't know it had happened, but now that I know she's like us, I can feel what that change in her was. Until yesterday, I thought her marrying the Gelus caused it."

Frowning, Maiçon stared through the flames at my wife. Considering his bite, I should say ours, but I didn't feel the same connection I did with Barden. By the morning after, our tri-bond had formed, and Barden and I were as connected as Sasha and me. I didn't feel that with

Maiçon, though. There was trust and a ready acceptance of him as a friend that wasn't there beforehand.

"When do you think it happened for her?" he asked.

"At a guess, after Sophie's funeral. I remember a sudden thunderstorm rolling in that afternoon. Savas was agitated when we got to his place, and Sasha couldn't be found. Barden brought her back later. That was the first time I noticed the difference, like a shadow looming around her. She went to the house, spoke to her grandmother, calmed down, and then went home with the Gelus."

Maiçon considered the information: "When I recognized her as a chosen one, I knew she was yours straightaway. I didn't know she'd married a Gelus first. Knowing it now, I think that bond-forming is why her awakening was much more subtle than ours. He kept her anchored, balanced the betrayal with his love and devotion."

Turning my gaze to his, I had to ask, "Why did you bite her? She's not your chosen one. The bond didn't form."

"She's not directly, no, but Sasha shares blood with the one who is," Maiçon answered. "And the bond is there; it's just not the same as a mate bond; it's a playful intimacy, almost like..." He drifted off, staring into the flames, a smile playing across his lips. "A best friend you flirt with, and everyone thinks you're fucking, but you don't, and you don't actually want to."

"So, you don't want to fuck her?" I checked. The feelings he just described were what I'd had with Sasha for the past twelve months, but the desire to fuck her had been there; it was just trumped by the need to see her happy and safe.

What I was starting to appreciate about Maiçon that Sasha had probably liked about him was that he took time to consider the truth before answering. "Not by herself, but if I were to bring her to bed with my chosen, I'd be into that." When I glared at him, Maiçon laughed. "I know it sounds weird, but that's the only situation I could fathom, and I think it has something to do with who my chosen is and her relationship with them."

"You think it's someone she shares blood with?" I checked.

"Yeah, her blood tasted right, but the bond, she wasn't my mate."

"Fuck, I hope it's not her mother."

"That would be awkward," Maiçon chuckled.

He didn't know half of it, considering how Delila felt about any species other than Orey.

Sasha stirred on the other side of the fire. I checked the horizon and pushed to my feet. "Sky is light enough to find our way back to the gate. Let's go." Moving around the fire, I stopped by Sasha as she wiggled into her clothes. Once covered, I offered her a hand and helped her to her feet. "Ready to go home?"

"Decidedly," Sasha sighed. "Please tell me you know the way."

That made me tilt my head. "Once a Gelus has flown somewhere, they can always find their way back. Doesn't that happen for you?"

"Yes, but I fell badly and then came to this beach from under the sea and was unconscious for most of that underwater travel," Sasha snarked. "Since you didn't stumble here, you're the tour guide."

"I know the way," Maiçon said. "I've been to Pandora plenty of times."

"Pandora?" Sasha asked. "As in the box from which all the world's evils were unleashed?"

"As in the realm that all matter of life as we know it, the good and the evil, was created," Maiçon corrected. Unfurling his yellow-gold wings, Maicon gave me a wink and launched into the sky.

"He's going to drive Barden insane," I muttered. "They both think they know it all."

Sasha gave me a teasing shove. "They are both quite a bit older than us. In comparison to our life experience, they do know it all."

The words were playful, but a shadow in Sasha's eyes as she looked back down the beach as if searching for someone made me worry about the sudden darkness of her aura.

"Everything alright?" I checked.

Bringing her gaze back to me, Sasha smiled. The shadows cleared as she tapped her shoulders and hips, changing into a top that would allow her wings to unfurl unhindered. Once her snowy feathers were displayed, we surged into the sky and followed Maiçon back to the gate.

Exiting the darkness into the cavern again was an eye-opener. Large spears of amethyst glowed in the darkness on the far wall, giving the cave an eerie aura. The fact that I'd all but killed my father in here didn't add to the atmosphere. Neither did the contingent of distrustful-looking Gelus, especially when those looks were coming at me.

"Sasha," Simon exhaled with relief when she stepped through beside me. "You're okay? Barden's been beside himself. Gavel had to come and force him to leave the caves to get some rest."

Sasha's eyes swung to me, and already I could feel her reaching out to our bond mate to assure him she was safe and coming home.

'I'm on my way. Be careful,' Barden warned. *'The others saw your eyes when you dealt with your father. They know.'*

I considered Hawk, Falco, and the other three friends they brought with them, and my eyes went to Simon, who was unsuccessful in moving Sasha away from me. She reached out for my hand and shifted right back in beside me.

Down the bond, I could feel her getting ready to expose herself, so I shut that down straight away. Squeezing her hand to get her attention, I gave a faint shake of my head. *'The only person you can tell is Barden—no one else. The Gelus regard female Narsitee as worse than the men. It would be a death sentence for you, for me, for Barden if they find out.'*

Trembling, Sasha cuddled into my side, a promise to keep her secret on the bond. Satisfied, I focused on the threat. "Are you going to hear my side at least, or are you just going to kill me right here and now?" I asked them.

Simon's eyes went from me to Sasha and back, and I understood they knew now she was my chosen one and that killing me required killing her. Yanking her behind me, I showed my teeth and snarled, "You will not hurt her."

Lifting his chin, Simon met my eyes. "We have no intention of hurting any of you. Lorka wants to see all of you, though. He has questions." Simon stepped closer. "I have questions."

Straightening up, I peered over my shoulder to my brother in warning. They wouldn't kill me because they cared about Sasha. She was one of them in their minds, but Maiçon didn't have that level of comfort. He needed to be careful. I met Simon's judgmental gaze again and said, "We'll come peacefully. You deserve an honest explanation, but Sasha will stay with me. Don't try to separate us. I only just got her back."

Nodding, Simon gestured to the exit and led the way, the other Gelus coming in behind us.

"I know you feel deceived, but nothing I said to you was a lie," I told Simon as we made our way through the caves. "I have Narsitee blood but am more like the Orey than my father."

"More Gelus," Sasha corrected. "You're not as closed-minded as the Orey and certainly nothing like your father. No offense, but he creeped me out at first sight."

"He has that effect on people," Maiçon grumbled. "What happened to the asshole?"

"He's dead," I answered.

Sasha turned to me and rubbed my arm. "I'm sorry. Finding out your dad was the one who killed Yasmine the way you did. I couldn't find an easier way to tell you, not with everything else happening."

Simon paused at the cave entrance and looked back at us. "Your father, that was the Narsitee in the cave that tried to kill your mum?"

"He was a hybrid," I explained. "Half Narsitee, half Gelus. Hence, I said I'm more Orey than anything. Half of my genes are Orey, while only a quarter are the others."

Flicking his eyes behind me, Simon jutted his head toward Maiçon. "And what about this kid?"

"My mother was a Gelus-Orey hybrid, so I'm more Gelus than anything," Maiçon answered without hesitation. "And I'm older than you by a good century."

Considering I knew Maiçon was a good three or more hundred years old, that took him out of the kid category. We'd gotten to know each other a little better on the trip back to the gate by playing twenty questions, and we realized how much we had in common, none of which related to our Narsitee powers.

"He's guilt-free, Simon," Sasha told him, her body pressing closer to my side as if she was afraid that the Gelus would try to take me from her. "They both are. I wouldn't be married to Vidal if he was like that. His morality is firmly intact."

Raising a brow at Sasha, Simon considered me, and then his eyes went to Maiçon again. "And that one?"

"Honestly, Barden is naughtier. Maiçon is a choir boy in comparison."

"I find that hard to believe. Barden has some of the most inflexible morals of any of us. The only reason we are even having this conversation is because Barden vouched for Vidal."

Speaking of Barden, he landed on the path ahead and stormed toward us. I could feel Sasha wanting to run to him, but she was unwilling to leave my side. Barden pushed past Simon and picked Sasha up in his arms, her hand still in mine as he kissed the fuck out of our wife.

"Never go underground again," Barden scolded Sasha when they broke for air. "Every time you're under the earth, you cause my heart to stop, and I must wait until you are above ground to breathe again."

Turning his gaze to me, Barden put his hand behind my neck and bowed our foreheads together. "Thank you for bringing our wife home, safe and unharmed."

I wanted to mention that I didn't think Sasha came home as unscathed as she seemed, but this wasn't the arena for such an admission. When Barden pulled back, his eyes went to my brother, and his jaw clenched.

"Maiçon saved me and nearly died protecting me there," Sasha told Barden tenderly. "He's no different from Vidal. He has morals and feelings, and he puts others before himself."

Not taking his eyes off Maiçon, Barden lifted his hand to Sasha's neck and caressed his thumb around the faded mark of my brother's bite. The grit of Barden's jaw as he did so was more than telling of his thoughts about Maiçon.

'The bond didn't take,' I told Barden. *'She's not his chosen. His pull to her was her blood connection to his chosen one.'*

'He still bit our wife and tried to claim her,' Barden argued.

'He did that to save me in case things went bad for Vidal,' Sasha confessed.

That made me pause and tilt my head. Barden didn't even need to think about it. *'In case his father killed Vidal, you had a better chance of surviving his death?'*

'And with my survival, Vidal had no risk of actually dying permanently.' Sasha confirmed.

"Are you done with this silent strategy meeting?" Simon asked. "Lorka has been waiting five days to deal with this matter."

"Five days?" I asked. "We were only gone for one night."

Simon raised a brow, but Barden said, "You've been gone for five nights. This is day six since you went through the gate."

"Fuck, no wonder Gavel had to force you to rest. I'm so sorry, brother," I pulled Barden into a one-armed hug, Sasha cuddling into both of us on the other side.

"You brought her back. That's all that matters," Barden said.

"No, it's not," Simon objected.

"Yes, it is." Barden turned on him. "She's the only thing that matters to me. Without her, I am nothing. She is my mate, my wife, my everything. Vidal is my brother-husband. You can't hurt him without taking Sasha from me, so stop trying to scare them because neither you nor any of them are going to raise a hand against an innocent girl just because you fear Vidal might be some psychopathic god. I think his actions over the last year have already proven he's not."

"Plus, it's well known that even a full-blooded Narsitee is calmer and more sympathetic when he finds and bonds with his chosen one," Maiçon added.

"They are?" nearly everyone present asked.

Frowning at the chorus of surprise, Maiçon moved closer to Sasha, obviously deciding no one would risk hurting her to kill him. "Yes. Whether male or female, a Narsitee becomes much less lethal once their bond with their chosen one is solidified. Unless the chosen one is killed, of course. If they survive the death, they tend to go nuts."

Maiçon eyed the others, but then his gaze trained on Simon. "That's why the females were wiped out. It took one losing her chosen one and going on a revenge-fueled world-domination bender, and the Gelus decided they were all power-hungry psychos and targeted them all. In truth, female Narsitees are pure empathy and logic. They were the good face of the gods, while the males were the wicked side of the coin."

Absorbing every word, Simon eventually huffed out a breath. "Lorka is waiting."

Without further argument, we were led to the top of the path, and then Simon demanded the keys to Maiçon's SUV. My brother took the passenger seat, and Barden and I put Sasha in the back seat between us.

Starting the engine, Simon lifted his eyes to the rearview mirror. "You've got until we get to the hall to convince me you are not a danger to our people. Make it good."

The Confession

SASHA

"HERE," Elisha handed me a can of lemonade as I tried to focus and stand up straight. Barden stood behind me, his arms around me, holding me tight, and Vidal held my free hand.

Simon was huddling with Lorka, revealing my knowledge of Vidal and Maiçon. Our word hadn't been enough. Still, I seemed more affected by the experience this time than the last two times. I just wanted to curl up in Barden's arms and sleep.

Simon turned his head and eyed me as they talked before looking back at Lorka. Whatever he said made Lorka blink and then look my way himself.

'Sasha,' Vidal worried in my head.

Unable to guarantee what Simon had seen through my eyes, I stayed quiet and drank my lemonade.

Down our bond, Barden alternated between giving assurances it would all be okay and asking what happened after I fell through the gate.

The side door opened, and my dad and Savas charged in, along with Nelly and Gavel. My father and twin immediately beelined for me. For the first time since I'd crossed the gate, my mates let go of their hold on me to let my family check on me and reassure themselves that I was okay.

As much as I wanted to tell them I was fine, I was so overwhelmed just to be here, to have survived that fall, to have come face to face with a true god, that I couldn't form words. Instead, I sobbed as I hugged them tightly.

Eventually, we pulled back, and as I went to step back, I ran into Maiçon, who was hovering over me now.

"Who's the Vidal Doppelganger?" Savas asked, eyeing Maiçon with curiosity. Dad's gaze was openly skeptical of the new guy.

"This is Vidal's half-brother, Maiçon," I introduced him. "Maiçon, this is my father, Gannix, and my twin brother, Savas."

"You have a twin?" Maiçon cocked a brow, and then his eyes were back on my brother again.

"Oh, shit," Vidal chuckled behind me.

"What'd I miss?" Barden asked, but after exchanging a look with Vidal, he put his fist to his mouth and cough-laughed into it.

"Well, this should be interesting," Maiçon muttered to himself.

That's when it clicked. I shared blood with Maiçon's chosen one. My eyes widened as I looked between them and double-blinked. "Oh..."

Cupping the back of my skull, Maiçon shook his head slightly, asking me not to say anything. Then, he kissed my temple and murmured, "Thank you." Stepping by me to stand with my brother, Maiçon took on a friendly tone and said to Savas, "I'm Vidal's half-brother on the Gelus side of his family. We only met a few days ago. Sorry, Raisa mentioned Sasha had an older brother, but not that you were twins. You look a lot alike. Do you like the same things?"

"You know Raisa?" Savas asked in surprise.

"We go to university together, and I've been tutoring her. That's how I met Sasha. She had lunch with us and then brought Vidal to meet me."

It was the truth, but it was also not quite the truth. My brother studied Maiçon briefly, blinked, and then looked at me. I shrugged. "That's pretty much what happened in a very refined summary. Maiçon saved my life on the other side."

"When you fell through the gate?" Savas asked.

"The gate that only Narsitee can activate?" My father added with an arched brow. Both their eyes fell on Maiçon with utter suspicion, then turned on Vidal.

Well, shit, I guess that cat was out of the bag. If the other Gelus knew, my father and Savas would probably have been informed.

"We were questioned extensively about Vidal and your relationship after your disappearance," my father told me quietly. His finger traced the scar of Vidal's bite, his eyes flaring with anger. Then his gaze found the newer set of faded teeth marks, and his eyes narrowed as they fell on Maiçon.

"He did it to save me. He's not my mate like Vidal and Barden," I assured.

When my father's gaze fell back on Maiçon, he met my father's steel gaze without flinching. "It's a mark of protection, not a romantic claim," he assured my dad.

Since my father and brother are like walking lie detectors, the fact that they both relaxed at Maiçon's answer also caused Barden to release a sigh of relief. He pulled me back against him a second later and nuzzled my neck.

"Well, that's good. I'd hate to think my daughter was gathering herself a harem."

I laughed. "No. So much no. I have only just got used to two; I couldn't fathom how three would work."

"I could send you links to some videos that might help," Savas offered with a wicked smirk.

My father gave him a playful shove. "Knock it off. Barden and Vidal have already corrupted her enough."

"Nowhere near enough, yet," both my mates whispered, making me squirm and blush.

A throat clearing made us all sober and give our attention back to my grandfather. "Based on what I've heard and what Simon could see from Sasha's interactions with Vidal and Maiçon, I agree that these hybrids are not like their Narsitee ancestors and appear closer to their Gelus kin in morals and personality. We'll accept them and watch closely to ensure no future deception."

The other Gelus present bowed their heads and headed outside. "Sasha, a word," Lorka called before we could follow. "Just Sasha," he clarified when my husbands and kin remained.

"No offense, Lorka," Barden replied, "but there is no chance we are leaving our wife's side right now. I just got her back."

Gesturing to Simon that he could go, Lorka met my eyes. "I just have a personal question for her. You can leave the door open so you can always see us if you feel threatened by me."

Squeezing Vidal's hand, I let it go. Barden was reluctant to release his hold, but I patted his hand and said, "It's okay. I'll be right out."

Grunting in my ear in his Neanderthal way, telling me he wasn't happy, Barden let go and left the hall with my kin and Vidal, leaving me alone with my grandfather.

We'd had several family dinners over the last nine months to get to know him better. Mum knew him from work and wasn't settled with the knowledge of him being Gelus, so she treated him as a colleague instead of family. It made the dinners funny for the rest of us.

"Sit with me for a moment, Sasha," Lorka gestured to the sitting area. We took seats, and then he took my hand, but I didn't miss how his pointer finger nestled above my pulse. "Don't be alarmed. I just had some follow-up questions for you, things I don't believe the others are ready to hear."

"Okay," I answered with a frown. I wasn't sure where he was going with this.

"Simon picked up some inconsistencies with what you heard and saw."

"Such as?"

"Maiçon told you only someone with Narsitee blood could operate the gate, that anyone not a Narsitee that passed through would die or become enthralled, yet you sit here whole."

Blinking at how easily I was exposed, I sat there speechless. Without realizing it, my hand came to my neck and traced the scars of the bites.

Tilting his head, Lorka watched my fingers. "You think the bond protected you?"

Chewing my lip, I thought about all the signs I'd inadvertently given away that Simon might have pieced together. Maybe the bond of being a chosen one could cover it all.

"When Vidal first marked me, Barden had me sit with him to question him. Being his chosen protects me from Vidal's manipulation and enables me to see when he's telling the truth. I think it works on more levels than that. I believe being chosen might protect me from all of them."

"How so?"

"At the cafe, Maiçon tried to use his power on me to get me to tell him things I refused. It worked a little, but I quickly cleared it away."

"And when Vidal tried to enthrall you, but the bond broke as soon as your lips parted, do you think that was the bond protecting you also?" Lorka asked.

"It would make sense. The bond makes me less susceptible to their power. It would be why the chosen ones were untouchable by the others. The bond protected them," I theorized.

Watching me, Lorka patted my head with his free hand, sweeping my hair back from my face and lifting my eyes to his with that motion. "After you dragged Maiçon ashore and realized he was close to death. Do you remember the beach in Pandora, Sasha?"

Lightning flashed behind my eyes, the tall, imposing figure in his cloak of darkness and a galaxy in his hood on a storm-swept beach.

"Shh, it's okay," Lorka cooed, my head against his chest as I breathed heavily.

Was I hyperventilating?

"Shh, I've got you."

"What did you do?" Barden asked through gritted teeth. I was pulled out of Lorka's arms and into his, Vidal right there, retaking my hand.

Getting to his feet, Lorka clasped his hands before him, his eyes all for me. I was still trying to calm my breathing, but my eyes stayed on my grandfather.

"Sasha has experienced significant trauma over the past twelve months," Lorka stated. "Simon noted it the last time he dragged her memories, but he is worried after this visit to her mind. Do yourselves a favor, get her to talk to you about whatever happened on that beach before Vidal found her, and if you are as worried as we are about her well-being, get her some therapy to deal with the trauma."

Lorka reached forward and patted my head again, keeping his voice low as he said. "And don't fret, my special granddaughter, I already knew of Eyal's origins. You have nothing to fear in me knowing it. Now go home; you have a new husband to settle in." With a kiss to my crown, he left us.

"Shit," Vidal muttered.

"What does he mean Eyal's origins?" Barden grumbled.

Sliding his gaze to where the others were still congregated outside, Vidal watched Lorka talking to Simon with their eyes still on me. "Not here. Let's take her home and follow her grandfather's advice. It will reveal his meaning on its own."

Huffing, Barden kept me tight to him as we made our way outside. When we arrived, Maiçon and Savas talked like old friends. My father came straight over. "Is everything okay?"

"Simon told Lorka that the trauma Sasha has experienced over the last twelve months has reached a breaking point. He wants her to deal with it in therapy," Vidal explained quietly.

I honestly didn't feel mentally vulnerable and thought I was coping with it all fine until he asked about the beach.

"I'll get some names and numbers for you," Dad offered with a caress to my cheek. "Let's take you home so you can rest." Pausing, he looked over his shoulder and cringed. "We only brought the bikes."

"We have Maiçon's car. He'll need to come back with us anyway to talk things through, but if it's okay, we'd like some time with Sasha before he comes up," Barden said.

"He and Savas are getting along well. I'm sure Sav will be happy to entertain him for a while," Dad assured. "I'll cook dinner and let you know when it's ready."

Reaching for my father's arm before he could turn away, I said, "We need to tell Grandma Tormen about Lorka. We can't keep segregating family dinners to hide him. If he wants to be part of our family, he must confront his part in it."

Putting his hand over mine, Dad gave it a gentle squeeze and then headed for his bike. "Sav, come on. Maiçon will follow us back with the rest."

Frowning, Maiçon wandered with us to his SUV. "I'm coming home with you?"

"You bit our wife, and the other Gelus know it," Vidal snarked quietly.

"Right," Maiçon replied, looking sheepish.

I tripped over my feet, and only Barden holding me around the waist stopped me from falling.

"I'm tired," I said in explanation.

"Understandable. We flew for nearly a day to get back to the gate, and you had an inquisitor in your head for a good hour," Maiçon said as he unlocked the car to let us all in.

"That took an hour?" I gasped.

"A little over," Barden gritted out. "Have some more lemonade when we get home."

Once we were in the car, Barden looked at me. "Tell me what Lorka meant about Eyal's origins."

Sighing, I leaned on his shoulder. "Eyal's gift is not from his Gelus blood, but rather that of his father. I met him on the beach in Pandora. He's a particular Narsitee whose powers were wrapped around death and a creature's soul. He's your distant kin, too. All the crows are his descendants, not just his creation."

The car was quiet, lulling me into a half-sleep state until Barden finally spoke. "Did this Narsitee tell you anything more, touch you in any way? Is that why Simon is worried about your trauma?"

That storm-ravaged beach blew through my mind again, the vast black wings of a god wrapping around me as he held me to him and imparted wisdom that should never have been mine upon my mind. Before he released me this time, I heard his voice one last time.

'Two pairs of twins. One is separated by centuries, and the other is bound never to be apart. All four bound to us by blood and power.'

Swallowing as my eyes flicked to Maiçon in the rearview mirror, I whispered, "He didn't hurt me. He just explained Eyal's gift to me." It was too late to change our fate. We were all bound together already. Fate had played its hand; we would have to take the ride whether we wanted to or not.

Breathing a breath of relief, Barden tucked me closer and kissed my crown. "No more, Sash. You've risked your life enough."

He had no argument from me. Assuring them down the bond that I wouldn't risk them or me any further, I closed my eyes and let the gentle motion of the car carry me into the sleep I needed.

The Tri-bond

SASHA

GOD, it was hot!

A tingle raced down my spine, a hand pressed against my rear and a deep mumble of hot breath against my ear.

Opening my eyes, my vision was filled with a bare muscular chest, a smattering of dark hair down the midline, through a valley of defined abs, before it disappeared beneath the sheet.

Tilting my head back, I smiled as I took in Vidal, still asleep, looking very delicious. Barden shifted behind me, his hard cock pressing between my butt crack, his fingers tensing over my abdomen as his mouth dropped to my shoulder and pressed a chain of kisses from the point to my neck.

"How are you feeling?" he mumbled.

Was there an answer to that? After everything I'd learned, it had been a hell of a year, that's for sure. I settled on, "Rested.".

"Good." Using his hand at my chin, he turned my face to his and pinched my lips, once, twice, then a third, much more passionate exchange.

The hand on my ass tensed, relaxed, and pulled away as Vidal rolled to his back and stretched. Barden slowed the kissing, and I cracked my eyes to see him peering at Vidal.

Sitting up, Vidal threw his legs off the bed and got to his feet, his boxers tenting around his erection. "I'm going to turn on the coffee machine and shower in my old room," Vidal stated with a yawn as he finger-combed his head and left the room.

I half sat up as the door shut, confused. I wasn't ready to be with both simultaneously, but I hated that he was leaving.

"Hey," Barden whispered, caressing my arm and returning my attention to him. "Vidal and I know you're not ready to be put between us. We'll let that intimacy build slowly, and when all three of us feel comfortable being intimate together, that will happen, but not yet. For now, Vidal will move into our room and sleep in here with us, but when one initiates intimacy, the other will find somewhere else to be and wait our turn."

"Is that fair?" I asked, letting Barden guide me back into his arms.

"It's fairer to me and Vidal than you."

"How's that?" I frowned, tilting my head and wondering how that wasn't fair to me.

Moving quickly, Barden flipped me onto my back and hovered above me. "Because you're going to be spending double the time you already do on your back getting your brains fucked out, that's how," he growled, then his lips smashed down on mine, and all thoughts of inequity and worry went right out the window.

Reaching between us, I slipped my hand beneath the waistband of his boxers and took Barden's cock in my palm, stroking it slowly as he kissed me intently.

Grunting, Barden lifted his weight onto his arms and shifted to hold himself with one hand as he started shoving his boxers out of the way. Helping him with my spare hand, I pushed them over his hips and used my feet to push them down his legs before Barden kicked them off.

"Fuck, Sasha, get naked already," he rumbled at me as his free hand shoved my top out of the way.

Closing my eyes, I clicked my fingers and gave Barden what he needed.

"I fucking love that ability of yours," he murmured as he covered my neck with kisses, then guided his seeping tip to my core. I was so wet and ready for him that Barden slipped straight into my opening, and then he slammed the rest of his length into me.

My back arched, and air rushed from my lungs from the force of his claiming me. My core spasmed from the sudden stretch as Barden held us like that for several long breaths.

"No more near-death experiences for me, Sash. I can't take that shit. Promise me." Barden asked, both of us panting against each other's mouths.

I wanted to promise him and myself, but the truth was, there was no such surety. "I promise I will be much more cautious and never knowingly walk into a dangerous situation without you next to me ever again."

Caressing my face, Barden stared into my eyes and smiled. "I'll take that."

"Now, please, fuck me," I pleaded, knowing how it got him going.

With a curse, Barden captured my mouth in a fiery kiss that zapped straight to my core, making me moan as he pulled back and then shoved deep into me.

"You are so fucking beautiful, Sash. Everything about you." Barden pulled out, then thrust back in savagely. "Your beauty, your personality, your kind heart, your power. There isn't anything about you that doesn't leave me in awe that you are mine."

"Ours!" Vidal yelled from the other room.

Barden smirked wickedly, and then he pounded into me over and over, claiming me with his usual savage possession. Quick and dirty wantonness rendering all sense of the outside world mute.

My body tightened without warning, and Barden cursed as he picked up the pace just before I screamed my orgasm. He cursed repeatedly as he found his release, and my body milked it from him.

Groaning, Barden dropped his head to my shoulder, biting it gently before he kissed and licked it better. "Mine. Ours. It's all the same. I love you, Sasha," he told me, breathing hard and his fingers caressing my ribs, the side of my breast.

"I love you too," I whispered.

The bedroom door opened, and Vidal sauntered in naked as the day he was born, his cock standing hard and tall. "Water is warm," he said, offering Barden a cup of coffee.

Huffing a laugh, Barden rolled to the side, then sat up and accepted the offering. "You're a kinky fucker."

Shrugging off the accusation, Vidal offered me the second cup. "I like her already dirtied up for me," he said without inflection. "But, dude, have you heard of foreplay? You will damage our girl if you don't get her motor revved for us first. Here, let me show you how it works."

Before I could object, Vidal slid his hand over my pussy and two fingers inside me. "Fuck!" I moaned, my head hanging back, and Vidal quickly rescued the cup of coffee I'd been holding from spilling all over me.

"I know how to do foreplay, you dick. I'll be in the shower," Barden snarled, but with a touch of a smile at the side of his mouth, then he walked his fine ass into our ensuite. "If I can't hear her screaming your name in here, then I'll take it you've done a shit job and come and finish her off for you."

"Fuck you. They'll hear her screaming for me in Valhalla," Vidal replied, just as his thumb worked my clit in small circles, and seconds later, I was calling his name. "Louder, baby. Make that crow hear you."

Falling to the bed, I smacked Vidal's shoulder with a laugh. He just fell over me, rolling me with him until I straddled his hips. Stilling for a moment, Vidal caressed my face. "Jokes aside, I'm with Barden on avoiding any more close calls, okay?"

"I have an easy solution. Take turns fucking me all day long, and I'll never get to leave the house to get in any danger," I sassed.

Grinning like a maniac, Vidal gripped my neck and pulled my mouth to be right above his. "Deal."

His kiss was challenging and demanding, which contradicted the featherlight way his fingers teased my nipple.

"Vidal," I moaned.

"Take me inside you, baby. I'm yours completely."

Lifting my hips, I sheathed his thick cock inside me, biting my lip on the stretch. I didn't think Barden and Savas were joking when they suggested a guy's wingspan was indicative of their dickspan.

"That's it," Vidal moaned as he helped press me down the length of him. "Take all of me, Sasha."

"Oh, god," I whispered as he filled me. Tingles raced up my spine, and my core tightened.

"That's it, baby . Now, look into my eyes," Vidal urged.

He waited until my eyes met his, then he smiled and pinched my nipple. At the same time he pulsed his cock inside me, making my back arch.

"Keep your eyes on me, Sash," he crooned.

Chewing my bottom lip, I met his gaze, and I swear the room grew ten degrees warmer.

"Now keep your eyes locked with mine and ride me, baby."

Pressed into my hands on his chest, I rose, then dropped down, curving my pelvis under as I lifted again, arching my back to lower. Our eyes stayed connected, and I found myself falling into him and that gaze until it was just Vidal and me. No one else mattered. No one else existed. It was just us, and our bodies joined repeatedly.

My climax built quickly, tightening my body and making me moan louder. As I reached the precipice, Vidal gritted his teeth and said, "That's it, baby. Come for me." He released my hip to palm my breast and pinch my nipple.

I tumbled, freefalling into the pleasure. Vidal strained under me, then he gave a yell of his climax and thrust up hard as his cock pulsed inside me. The pressure of his release took my orgasm to the next level.

"Vidal!" I called as I threw my head back, riding him until my climax petered out, and then I sagged on top of him, nibbling and kissing his neck in worship.

"Fuck, baby, you fuck mean for an innocent thing."

Frowning, I raised enough to peer down at Vidal to see what he meant. He chuckled as he pointed to the red nail marks across his chest.

"They're not bleeding; stop complaining," I teased, then fell to the side.

"Is it my turn?" Maiçon asked.

Yanking the sheet to cover me, I crunched to see him leaning against the bedroom door jamb. "How long were you standing there?"

"What the fuck!" Vidal yelled. "Who let you in?"

"Chill, I waited outside until you finished. Savas had to go to soccer training. He told me to head up so we could talk before dinner."

Cursing under his breath, Vidal sat up, grabbed the coffee from the bedside table, and gestured to his brother. "Shut the door. We'll be out in a few."

Giving me a wink, Maiçon shut the door. I collapsed back on the bed with a huff. "How is this going to work?"

Vidal sipped the coffee, offered it to me, and helped me sit back up with his other hand. His fingers caressed my spine as I accepted the wake-up juice, but his fingers tangled in my hair and forced my mouth to his for a passionate coffee-flavored kiss first.

"We're going to shower, then, ask Maiçon what he wants and see if that fits with us. If it does, we make room for him," Vidal informed.

"How can Savas be his chosen one if they are both into women?" I questioned.

Vidal lifted a brow and then a shoulder. "Maybe they aren't entirely straight. Maybe there is just enough flexibility in their orientations that connects them. I don't know. As you got older, I questioned you being my chosen one, but you turned out perfectly for me."

"Why did you question it?"

Smirking, Vidal stole the rest of the coffee back and drank it. "I knew I was into... let's say, spicy sex by the time I was sixteen. You were so damn innocent, Sash. When you hit sixteen and still came off as a good girl, I questioned how we could be meant for one another. Though, I admit I loved the idea of dirtying you up. I never expected it to happen once Barden was on the scene, and I fully expected him to corrupt you. But he didn't. You could still role-play an angel for us with little effort."

"For crying out loud, can you let the Angel roleplay go already?" I scolded, rolling my eyes.

That just made Vidal laugh. He set the mug aside, then hauled me off the bed and over his shoulder as he cracked a smack against my naked ass. "Let's get you cleaned up."

Vidal took me into the ensuite and set me down right outside the shower. "Maiçon's here," he told Barden.

Taking my wrist, Barden pulled me into the shower with him. "I hope he's comfortable. We're going to be a little longer."

Before I could object, Barden crushed his mouth down on mine as he lifted me to his waist and pressed me back against the wall.

Vidal sighed and chuckled. "Make it quick. I'll strip the bed. We made a mess of the sheets."

Ignoring him, Barden thrust into me and wasted no time having me cry out his name again. If the boys kept this up, I'd be walking funny for the rest of the week.

We eventually cleaned up and made it out to the lounge room. When we came out, Maiçon sat there drinking a beer and watching The Witcher.

"Make yourself at home," Barden grumbled.

"You're the ones too busy fucking to pay attention to your guests," Maiçon replied. His eyes came to me and lit up. "Not that I can blame you."

"Stop looking at our wife like she's your personal porn show," Vidal scolded. "She's not your chosen one."

Shrugging it off, Maiçon grabbed the remote and turned the television off. "So, fam, what are we talking about?"

"The Gelus think you bonded with Sasha," Vidal stated.

"I did bond with her, just not like you did," Maiçon debated.

"It might be the only reason they didn't kill you," Vidal pressed. "So, we can't ignore your mark on her and pretend it never happened."

Maiçon flinched. "Right, so we have to keep up appearances."

"Maybe. What are you hoping for?" Vidal asked as we all settled into the long sofa. Barden sat on one side of me, Vidal on the other, so we could face Maiçon in the armchair.

"I want to get to know my chosen one. This isn't what I expected, so I want to explore this slowly." Maiçon mussed his hair with his hand as he shook his head.

"So, you're not into guys?"

"I wasn't," Maiçon answered with a chuckle. "Though, your brother is hot."

"He also has a Gelus mate," I warned.

That made Maiçon pause. "Are they mated?"

"Not yet," Barden grumbled.

Maiçon blinked at Barden, and when his eyes came to me, I shrugged and whispered, "His mate is Barden's older sister."

"Fuck me," Maiçon muttered.

Barden grunted and leaned back to put his arm over my shoulders as he turned to meet Vidal's eyes. He gave Vidal a subtle nod, then leaned into me and kissed my neck.

"Where are you living?" Vidal asked.

"I have a dorm room on campus. I plan on finishing my degree, so, for now, I can live there. Maybe I can crash here on weekends and get to know Savas better?"

"Sounds like a plan. You can take my old room," Vidal decided as he got to his feet. "But you will respect our privacy and not come waltzing in on us in bed."

"As if that bothered you," Maiçon teased.

Shaking his head, Vidal tilted his head my way. "Sasha is the definition of innocent."

"I'm not that innocent anymore," I muttered, rolling my eyes. This made all three of them snicker.

"Let me rephrase. Sasha has only just accepted having two husbands physically. If you make her uncomfortable in her own home, I will drop-kick you off the balcony, and you won't be welcome back."

"I'll behave," Maiçon assured.

"Probably better than you ever did," Barden teased Vidal.

"She is my chosen. For that fact alone, I was very patient." Grabbing my jacket off the back of the lounge, Vidal held it for me. "I guess Maiçon should come to dinner and meet your mother."

"Oh, boy. If you tell her I've married him too, she will literally lose her shit."

"Which will be better, me married to you or your brother?" Maiçon asked seriously.

Barden, Vidal, and I cringed. The Orey were not very open-minded.

"Perhaps, for now, we introduce Maiçon as your half-brother whom you only just met, and we leave the intricacies of bonds and chosen ones out of it," Barden suggested.

Pointing at my gorgeous husband, I said, "Best idea. Vidal's brother. That will do us. By the way, how is Helena?"

"I called her while you were sleeping. She's okay. Shaken, but more worried about you than she was about me," Vidal told me as we headed down to the house in the elevator.

"It's only fair she likes me better than you since my mother likes you more than me," I teased.

"I could fix that," Barden muttered, making Vidal and me laugh.

We piled onto the elevator, and then Barden looked at Maiçon. "Can you cook?"

"Not really."

"Learn. We share the chores in our home."

"I will spend my night looking up cooking know-how," Maiçon assured.

Barden gave him a grunt, then wrapped me in his strong arms and nuzzled my neck. "Stop bringing strays home; this elevator has reached maximum capacity."

Smiling to myself, I reached out and pulled Vidal to my front and kissed him, long and slow. My men groaned. Barden's lips pinched my ear lobe on one side, and Maiçon mimicked him on the other as he whispered. "Watching the three of you gets me hard."

Turning my face towards him, I cuffed the back of his neck and planted a kiss on his lips. Two seconds later, the door flew open, and Maiçon was expelled from the elevator by Barden's hand.

Luckily, we were nearly at the endpoint, so he only fell a meter to the ground.

"Message received," he groaned from where he lay, causing the three of us to burst out laughing.

The Epilogue

VIDAL

SIX MONTHS LATER

THE BEDROOM DOOR opened and closed. Lifting my head from the pillow, I watched Barden move across the room for the shower. There was blood down one side of his face, and I had no doubt his clothes were drenched as well. I'd felt it down the bond when he'd run into an aggressor last night. Sasha had been giving me the world's best blow job and pulled off me while she focused on our bond mate's rage. I swear the fucker did that shit just to cockblock me sometimes.

Turning my focus to the girl in question, who was using my chest as her pillow, I ensured the blankets were tucked around her, keeping her warm. She had one of Barden's shirts on, but that's it. She rarely wore pajamas inside the bedroom anymore. She preferred our shirts, and we preferred her naked, so this was the compromise.

Coming from the bathroom, freshly showered and in his boxers, ready for bed, Barden studied Sasha, the way she was sprawled across me like I was a teddy bear, then lifted his eyes to mine. *'Nightmares again?'*

'Just the one,' I told him.

It had taken months for Sasha's nightmares to die down after Yasmine's death, only for the Pandora Gate experience to give her new ones. Worse ones. The way Sasha would scream in these nightmares would bring Maiçon running from the other end of the house. Sometimes, he was the only one who could wake her from them.

One reason Maiçon gave up his dorm room and moved in with us permanently was so he could be here to help Sasha through that trauma. The other, as it turned out, was that he couldn't stomach being away from her for too long. Barden attributed it to the same way Sasha and Savas couldn't stand to be parted too long, and we suspected it had something to do with their bond.

'Was Maiçon needed?' Barden queried as he slid into bed behind Sasha. The ones that required Maiçon were about falling from the gate and how Sasha had had to drag his broken body from the surf.

'No, it was a mild one. Just the Narsitee on the beach.'

Those didn't make her scream. She would struggle as if she was being held against her will and mutter, "I don't want to know this," under her breath repeatedly.

At first, we worried the Narsitee had physically assaulted Sasha, but she assured us that he hadn't harmed her. Still, whatever had occurred had traumatized her to the same level as falling to her death and watching Maiçon be broken and killed on the way down.

Maiçon could only tell us his part, and when Sasha wouldn't tell us what happened on that beach, Barden went to Simon for answers. Unfortunately, other than Sasha encountering a very old and powerful Narsitee, he couldn't tell us anything.

Since Maiçon had a psych degree, he was the backup, on-call therapist, but because he was part of Sasha's trauma, he told us straight away that she needed an outsider to confide in.

Barden didn't give Sasha a choice after that. He made her an appointment with a psychologist specializing in trauma and took her to each appointment personally, so she had to show up. It helped, but Sasha was still healing.

When she was awake, however, you wouldn't know she spent her nights watching her friends die and experiencing it firsthand. I worried that Sasha had accepted those nightmares as her everyday existence, or that she had some severe compartmentalization happening.

Most days, Sasha was happy, focused on her studies, and regularly spent time out of the house with her brother and Raisa. Maiçon always tagged along when he could with those two. The trauma certainly wasn't affecting Sasha's sexual appetite either.

The sex was often and phenomenal. I wasn't tempted by anyone else at all anymore. The only woman I wanted was my wife, and I was up for it every time she even looked at me sideways. I'd never been happier. If we could get Sasha past this last trauma and have her sleeping soundly again, I'd be the happiest man in the world. For now, every night brought with it the concern for Sasha.

Cuddling in beside Sasha, Barden ran his hand up her spine. Sasha shifted her lower body so she could press against him and moaned his name.

Kissing her temple, I started to slip out of bed to give them private time. That's how it had worked for the last six months. Sasha and I utilized the time Barden was at work, and then I made myself scarce when he got home to let them be alone. The time we were both home was a first-in, first-served situation—literally, in some cases.

"Stay," Sasha mumbled as I tried to move away, her arm tensing around me.

"Sash—" I tried to explain, but she cut me off.

"I want both of you," she said, voice a little bit less sleepy. "Together."

Don't get me wrong, Barden and I had been happy with the arrangement for the last six months, and neither of us had pressured or suggested we try being together with her; it was a decision Sasha had to make, when or if she was ever interested.

"Baby, open your eyes and look at me. We need to know you are awake and aware of what you're asking for before we act on it," I told her.

Grumbling under her breath, Sasha pushed up to hold herself on her elbows and opened her beautiful heterochromic eyes to meet mine. "I'm ready to be intimate with you both at the same time. Just to be clear, I am not proposing anal. I'd like you to share like we've been doing, just with you both staying in the room..." Sasha frowned, squinted one eye, then blushed and tried, "And assisting?"

I choked down a laugh. Bless her soul, she tried, but Sasha couldn't talk dirty and not come off as a virgin trying to portray a wanton woman. Even Barden turned his head to hide his smirk. It was cute and something we both loved about her.

Huffing, Sasha flipped over onto her back in annoyance and said, "Stop laughing at me and fuck me already."

"Well, when you ask so nicely," I teased, finding her thigh under the blanket and sliding my hand under her shirt.

Meeting my eyes, Barden gave one of his caveman grunts, and I smiled, understanding the demand.

Leaning towards him, Sasha kissed his bicep, her fingers tracing the definition of his shoulder muscles. "Please, fuck me, Barden. Please let Vidal stay and help."

The side of Barden's mouth twitched, and then he squirmed down under the blankets, spread Sasha's thighs open, and made her moan his name. Shoving her shirt up to her neck, I cupped one of her breasts in my hand, then attacked the other with quick sucks and flicks until Sasha had her fingers in my hair and cursing as she came for our mouths.

Kissing up her neck, I nibbled the lobe of her ear, then murmured, "I want you to suck my dick while Barden fucks you."

"Oh, god, yes, please!"

I laughed at Barden's cranky expression when she used the G word, but the rush it gave me every time Sasha said it was the equivalent of going to Sunday mass, and I wasn't going to give that up.

As Sasha lowered her face to pleasure me, Barden grabbed her hips and buried himself deep, making her cry out for him. I fisted her hair and held her away while Barden got those first few thrusts out of the way, then I guided Sasha to me, and for the first time, she pleasured both her husbands simultaneously. It was worth waiting for. Hell, we should have declared a public holiday in honor of it, it was so damn impressive.

When Barden had made her sing his name and filled her with his cum, I rolled her onto her back and pounded her until it was my name she worshipped, and then I claimed her right back.

Afterward, we lay spent, slick with sweat, and quiet together. We stayed that way until Maiçon slid the door open, stretching, yawning, and looking us over with a lazy smile. "Are we running, or are you all worn out from the fuckfest?"

"Fuck off. I can still outrun you," Barden grumbled and lobbed a pillow at him, taking satisfaction when it made Maiçon double over with an 'oof'.

"We'll rinse off. Why don't you make yourself useful and start making coffee?" I said as I moved towards him, shoved him back out of the room, and shut the door again. "See what happens when you bring strays home, baby?"

The nickname Barden had given Maiçon had stuck. Maiçon didn't mind; he actually laughed at it.

"You better all be on your best behavior at dinner tonight," Sasha warned, pulling Barden's shirt back on for the dash to the bathroom. "It's already going to be tense as it is."

"Baby, your grandma loves us. Even the stray has won her over. If anything, we'll make her first time seeing Lorka again bearable."

"You know I have the power to make her young again," Maiçon said through the door. "Grandma Tormen could relive her twenties, and she and Lorka could have another fifty years together."

"I believe she declined your offer already," Sasha reminded him.

"Yeah, but that was when I offered to make her my concubine. If it's for Lorka, she might be keen."

Huffing, Sasha leaned against the bathroom door. "I seriously don't think I could handle my grandmother suddenly being the same age as me. That would just be weird." Waiting until she heard Maiçon in the kitchen, Sasha lowered her voice. "She wouldn't, would she?"

Stopping in front of her, Barden grunted a 'fuck no', before stepping into the bathroom.

Cupping her face in my hand, I rubbed our noses together and murmured, "There is no chance. Your grandmother has made peace with her age. She doesn't wish to be immortal or even to live another lifetime. Barden explained to Melisandre that when she dies, Lorka can visit her in the afterlife, and they can be lovers there for eons instead. That was much more appealing."

"Do not encourage her to kick the bucket, either. Seriously, guys, I need her around for a long time yet. She always takes my side and gives Delila a hard time. It's almost my sole reason for living."

Laughing at Sasha's tease, I yanked her into the bathroom with me, pulling her under the water and sandwiching her between Barden and me. She was still in his tee, but as Barden kissed her slow and passionately, I used the thin, wet material to tease her nipples before we forgot about the run and lost ourselves in each other instead.

The Stray & the Twins

SASHA

ANOTHER SIX MONTHS LATER.

"COME ON, Baby. We'll be late for the run."

Energized upon waking, I slipped out of bed, used the bathroom, and dressed for our morning run. Vidal was already up making coffee, and Barden wasn't home yet.

"Is he not ready yet?" I asked Vidal when Maiçon wasn't there.

"Nope, but I've heard movement sounds from his room, so I know he's awake."

Typically, Maiçon was the first one up for a run in the morning, as long as my nightmares didn't call him in the middle of the night. Those nights, we both ended up exhausted. I don't know what it was about those memories of us falling that took so much out of me, but they did the same to Maiçon.

It had gotten better over the last year, the nightmares few and far between now. Soon, I'd only get them when triggered, like I did for Yasmine or Sophie.

"I feel full of energy this morning," I told Vidal as I bounced, keen to get out on the run.

Tilting his head, Vidal studied me. "You feeling okay, baby?"

"Yes, I feel great." Getting sick of waiting, I huffed, picked up Maiçon's coffee, and headed down the hall. "I'll go drag him out here."

"Sash—" Vidal tried to call me back, but I was already skipping down the hall.

"Come on, slow coach," I said as I opened his door, the same way he always entered our room without knocking.

My feet stopped, my jaw dropped, and I stared wide-eyed as my words and sudden arrival caused the three naked bodies on the bed to dive for cover, yanking up blankets. Okay, my brother and Calliope tried to cover it up.

"Fuck, Sash, I can explain," Savas worried, pleading for me to not be angry with him. I wasn't. I was happy for them. I would prefer not to see what I just did again.

Putting his hand on my brother's shoulder, Maiçon kissed his cheek and said, "She's fine, Sav. Don't fret."

Getting off the bed, butt naked, sporting a giant hard-on wrapped in a condom and glistening with lube, Maiçon sauntered over to me with the biggest smile on his face. "Morning, Sasha," he greeted, taking his coffee and kissing my lips. He always kissed me like that in front of others.

"You're okay with your husband being with others?" Savas asked, astounded.

"It's a bit late to worry about your sister's marriage now, Sav," Calliope lectured, rolling her eyes. "However, I will say none of us planned this, and we probably haven't considered the repercussions yet. Caught up as we were." Giving me an apologetic look, she shrugged.

Putting a hand on my hip, Maiçon walked me back a few steps, then nuzzled my neck and murmured, "I'm running late. Get started. Savas and I will catch up."

"With the run?" I whispered back.

"Hmm, that too," he replied cheekily. "Unless you want to join in?"

"Dude, she's my sister," Savas complained at the same time Vidal growled, "I will kill you. Brother or not."

Vidal was right behind me, his arm wrapping around my waist and gently urging me backward. "It looks like you're enjoying yourself, so take your time, and we'll go for a longer run."

As we returned to the kitchen, Vidal bent his knees to be at eye level with me. "Are you okay?"

"Did you know?"

"That he was fucking your brother and his girl? No. That he was fucking someone, yes," Vidal told me with a slight wince. "I did try to warn you."

"Yeah," I said, taking a breath. "Let's get him a lock for his door. Maybe we can get one, too."

Vidal smirked. "We can do that, but I doubt he'd use it, and a lock won't keep him out of our room. It would just be a placebo for your sensibilities."

"Okay, I understand, but my sensibilities just saw my brother getting plowed while he plowed, and they are a little traumatized, so we'll take the placebo, please."

Barely stopping from laughing at me, Vidal pulled me in against him and kissed me. "Are you sure you want to run? We could go back to bed and burn your energy right down in the best way."

Taking a breath, I pretended to consider the option. "I'll still need the run, but I guess it won't hurt to wait another hour or two," I decided, then squealed as Vidal tossed me over his shoulder and hauled me back to our bedroom.

The End.

Join the Beautiful and Deadly

Join Ebony's Mischief List

Sign up to Ebony's mailing list for the following perks:

- latest news on new releases
- heads up on upcoming promotions
- first chance at Giveaways
- get a free book

Go to https://ebonyolson.com for more information

Romance Suspense by Ebony Olson

Hotel Series

HOLLY CLAIRE TRILOGY

Best Sunrise: Books 1-3 Hotel Series

(Omnibus of Henderson, Cassidy, & Holmes)

JESS BUTLER TRILOGY

Best Sunset: Books 4-6 Hotel Series

(Omnibus of Best Man, Best Layover, & Best Knight)

Black Mark Series

Black Mark: The Complete Saga

(Omnibus of Resistance, Secret, & Heart)

Black Mark X

Standalone Books

Calypso

Rain: A Dark Past Romance

Protective Instinct (On KU as Hunter Enemy & Lover Enemy)

Dark Romantasy / Paranormal Romance by Ebony Olson

STANDALONE BOOKS

Of Shadow and Light

Boundary

Silver Rogue

Halos

The Grave Keeper: All Hallows

ANGELIS SERIES

Spectra

Angelis

HIERARCH SERIES (DARK ROMANTASY)

Succumb

Numinous

Masked

Exodus

Burning Immortality

OREY GELUS SERIES

Gelus Hearts (Compilation of Orey Witches & Edge Gelus)

Vidal

CHAOS STAR TRILOGY (SCI-FI ROMANCE)

Praldia

Cyra

Avalonia

Ebony lives in Sydney, Australia, with her husband, daughter, and six rescue cats. She loves to read fantasy, thrillers, and paranormal romance, spending most of her free time with her nose in a book or writing.

Having always possessed an over-active imagination Ebony spent her younger years regaling friends with fantastic stories, holding her audience captive with the passion and suspense of her characters plights. In adulthood, she shows no signs of stopping her imagination from spreading across as many pages as it can find.

Website: http://ebonyolson.com/
Ebony's Mischief & Mayhem Peeps

facebook.com/EbonyOlson.Author

instagram.com/ebony_olson

amazon.com/author/ebonyolson

bookbub.com/authors/Ebony_Olson

goodreads.com/Ebony_Olson

tiktok.com/@ebony_olson